"I think you're a bunch of phonies," Monique said. "It's a phony club based on a phony idea that handwriting reveals character." She picked up the dish of mints that Vonnie had placed on the table. "And the biggest phony of all is your leader. Just look at this, kids, *candy*!"

"We've all seen candy before," Dick said.

"And so has Vonnie Morrison! She's trying to fool you all with her poor-little-sick-girl act! Diabetics can't have candy. If Vonnie were really suffering from diabetes, she wouldn't even have candy in the house to tempt her!"

Monique set the candy dish back on the table. "Come on, gang!" She snapped her fingers and winked. "Let's get out of here and really have some fun!"

Vonnie was speechless. She could barely control her urge to throttle Monique Wager.

The Right Kind of Girl

DOROTHY FRANCIS

Keepsake
FROM
CROSSWINDS

≡≡≡ CROSSWINDS

New York • Toronto • Sydney
Auckland • Manila

First publication June 1987

ISBN 0-373-88001-4

RL 5.2, IL age 10 and up

Dear Reader:

Welcome to Crosswinds! We will be publishing four books a month, written by renowned authors and rising new stars. You will note that under our Crosswinds logo we are featuring a special line called Keepsake, romantic novels that are sure to win your heart.

We hope that you will read Crosswinds books with pleasure, and that from time to time you will let us know just what you think of them. Your comments and suggestions will help us to keep Crosswinds at the top of your reading list.

Nancy Jackson

Senior Editor
CROSSWINDS BOOKS

One

Monique pulled her pillow over her head as she heard her alarm ring, trying to ignore the sound. Monday morning! Who needed it! School! Who needed that! She wished someone would invent something for kids to do besides going to school. Or working. There ought to be other alternatives. She groped until she touched the cold silver of the alarm, then shut it off.

"Monique, are you awake?" It was the housekeeper, Glady. Her voice seeped through the closed door, through the pillow, through Monique's determination to ignore it.

"No. I'm still asleep." Superdumb questions rated superdumb answers.

"It's past seven," Glady called. "Time you were up and at 'em."

"I'm skipping school today," Monique mumbled. "I feel rotten. Headache. Sore throat."

"May I come in?"

"No. I might be contagious."

Glady opened the door and stepped into Monique's bedroom. Although the golden carpeting muffled her footsteps, Monique knew she was there. She could feel Glady watching her, and she flung off the pillow and forced herself to sit up. The pink satin quilt had slid to the floor, and Glady picked it up and laid it across the foot of the water bed before she handed Monique her silver-backed hairbrush.

"Your mother said to tell you you may drive her Mercedes this morning. Your father's taken your Camaro in for a tune-up."

Monique laid the hairbrush beside her, enjoying the gentle roll of the bed. "No, Glady. I'm not going to school today. I hate Mondays."

"Get with it, Monique. You can't skip school. Your mother said—"

"A lot my mother cares about my attendance!" Monique rammed her warm feet into cool satin slippers that matched her bedspread and shuffled to her walk-in closet.

"Of course she cares!"

"Wrong. She doesn't care about anything but her committees and getting her picture in the paper as she pours tea at some of her do-gooder charity affairs. Exclusive affairs, of course. If Mom actually saw a charity case, she'd probably barf from the shock of it. Face it, Glady. Mom's not into reality."

"You know that isn't true, Monique. Your mother does care about your attendance and your grades. Try to see her point of view. Corporate wives are expected to assume certain social duties—responsibilities—whether or not they enjoy them."

"She enjoys. Believe it. You heard it here first. She enjoys. It's totally gross."

"Sometimes a husband's promotions may depend on his wife's social abilities. Both your parents are busy people."

"Too busy for me," Monique muttered as she looked at the clothes jammed in her closet.

"Not so, Monique. Not so."

"I haven't even seen Dad for over a week."

"He's had business conferences."

"He spent the whole weekend playing golf in Dallas."

"Lots of business is conducted on a golf course, Monique. Try to understand."

"I understand that he's usually left for his office before I get up."

"He works hard for his family."

"If someone said, 'Guess who's coming for dinner,' Dad would be my last guess. We almost never eat together. And I'm in bed before he comes in at night. If he's so interested in me and so worried about his corporate image, how come he doesn't let me have just one wild new outfit? What will his peer group think if they see me running around looking like Raggedy Ann!"

Glady stepped closer to the closet. "You've got plenty of clothes. So get dressed."

Satin swished against satin as Monique pulled out a scarlet dress with a flared miniskirt, a blue crepe jumper, a brown suit with silk cuffs and collar. "Lovely in Paris, maybe, but they're the pits in Houston. They're not what the gang's wearing. It blows my mind that we have to live part-time in Paris, part-time in Houston. Why can't we just live like ordinary people?"

Ignoring the question, Glady pulled out a navy blue skirt and a ruffled white blouse. "Maybe these would do. They're sort of basic."

"Those kinds of ruffles aren't basic, Glady. Be real." She patted her hips. "Maybe if I lost ten pounds I could wear some of last year's Houston clothes."

"If you want me to, I'll figure out a low-cal diet for you," Glady offered.

"One of your if-it-tastes-good-spit-it-out diets?"

"Twelve hundred calories, maybe. That and a bit of exercise would help you take off a few pounds. You might try a three-mile walk after school."

"I'm not into walking."

"It would only take forty-five minutes or so. You could probably see a difference even before Christmas."

"Is that the way you keep so slim, Glady?" Monique smiled for the first time that morning. "I thought it was written somewhere that all good cooks are supposed to be fat."

"I haven't time to get fat. How about trying a diet? I could work in some of the things you really like."

"Forget it already, but thanks." Monique laid the blue-and-white outfit on her bed and began brushing her hair, wincing at the touch of the stiff bristles. "If I didn't pretend I loved those yucky French fashions and pretend that I'd hate being seen in anything else, my life would be total disaster. I'd be the laughingstock of Memorial High."

"Nobody's laughing at you, Monique."

"As it is, I think some of the kids see through my act. Vonnie Morrison for one. Sometimes I don't think I fool Vonnie about anything."

"Why would you want to?"

"Why *wouldn't* I want to?" She slammed the hairbrush onto the bed. "She's given me a hard time ever since we got back from Paris. First with Randy. Then with the shoplifting initiation for the Super Seniors club. It's really time I showed her who's leading the pack."

"I could lend you some money for a new outfit," Glady offered, changing the subject. "You could pay me back whenever you..."

"Whenever I finish paying off Neiman-Marcus?" Monique scowled. "That debt has me totally climbing the walls."

"Sorry I reminded you of it."

"It's the pits that I have to pay for every last little thing I sto...took." She couldn't bear to say the word "stole." Although she still preferred to think of shoplifting as a game, she knew it wasn't. The security officer at Neiman's had made that quite clear. "After all, I didn't keep the swimsuits and beach robes for myself. I gave them to Vonnie Morrison and her friends."

"And the kids returned them to you," Glady reminded her. "That was generous of them."

"Yeah. Real big of them."

"Surely you can understand that Neiman's can't sell used garments. You were lucky to be able to place them at Second Time Around. They'll surely sell there. Eventually, if you're patient, you'll get some money for them."

"A pittance." Monique sprayed gardenia cologne on her wrists, inhaling the sweet scent. "Cass Diedrich told me how those nearly new stores scam you. They put super low prices on really neat stuff, then when it sells, the store keeps half the money and the other half goes to the owner of the clothes. It's a real rip."

"Seems fair enough to me," Glady said. "Stores have a lot of overhead. It takes money to pay for electricity, sales clerks, rent."

"But if stuff hasn't sold after a month, then the manager cuts the price in half."

"That seems in line. She has to keep the merchandise moving, especially when that merchandise is used clothing.

If she didn't, the place would soon look like a rummage sale."

"But people deliberately *wait* for the markdown," Monique said. "Cass says she gets lots of neat stuff that way. There's a date on the sales tag and she figures out the exact day a garment will go on half price, then she zooms in on it like a vulture."

"Everyone waits for sales," Glady said. "It's a national pastime."

"Not me," Monique said. "If I like something, I buy it on the spot. Or at least I used to before Dad cut off my allowance."

"It'll all work out for the best." Glady plumped Monique's pillow and smoothed the rumpled case.

"Even if Second Time Around sells the things, and even if Dad gives me back my allowance to make the Neiman payments, I won't have the debt paid off until after the first of the year, and this is only November. What a drag! How am I going to get through the holidays?"

"I said I'd lend you enough to buy something new."

"Dad would kill me if he found out. You've heard about the iron hand in a velvet glove, haven't you?"

Glady nodded and began making the bed.

"Well Dad lost his velvet glove a long time ago. If I come up with one new item before that debt is paid off, I'll be on the endangered species list."

"Get dressed," Glady said. "Maybe you'll get some new jeans and sweaters for Christmas."

"And this is only November." Monique scowled as she buttoned the ruffled blouse and tucked it into the band of the French-style skirt. "But thanks for the offer, Glady." She smelled talc as she gave the housekeeper a hug, then in a burst of generosity she helped her finish making the bed. Glady was her friend. Glady understood her, most of the time. Frequently she felt as if Glady and her husband, Herman, were her only friends in the whole world. Sometimes she wished they were her parents, but she also felt sorry for them.

"Glady?"

"What?"

"Don't you ever get bummed out at doing chores nobody else wants to do?"

"I like cooking and keeping this house, Monique. Your parents have such beautiful things that it's a joy to take care of them."

Glady sounded sincere. She and Herman seemed quite happy living in the caretaker's cottage. Of course they had the use of the grounds, a car and the pool during the six months the Wagars were in Paris. That wouldn't be too hard to take. Maybe the fringe benefits made the job worthwhile.

After she was dressed, Monique gulped orange juice and toast, choking a bit on the last crust as she grabbed the keys to the Mercedes and headed for Randy Morrison's house. She and Randy had a deal. She picked him up one day and he picked her up the next. She wondered if Vonnie Morrison had ever driven Randy to school during the time they had dated before she returned from Paris. She wondered a lot of things about Vonnie Morrison. No doubt she had made a big thing of her and Randy having the same last name. It was probably how she trapped him into going out with her in the first place.

She turned the radio up full blast and tooted the horn once as she stopped in front of Randy's house. The front door opened immediately. Prompt. That was Randy. She liked to think of him waiting for her. What a hunk! He looked the part of a jock with his broad shoulders and narrow hips. His brown sweater and cords gave him a casual look Monique liked.

"Hi!" she yelled above the sound of the radio as he opened the door and slid onto the passenger seat. "Ready for another week?"

"Right!" Randy yelled back. "Ready and eager. But what about a movie tonight? I mean if someone doesn't assign a test for tomorrow."

"Sounds okay. But I've got another idea."

"Give."

"We could rent a movie cassette, invite a bunch of kids in, and show the movie on our VCR at home."

"What about your folks?" Randy asked. "Would they mind all the noise?"

"They're usually out." She tuned The Heartbreakers down a few decibels. "Anyway, they wouldn't mind. And Glady would make refreshments for us. How about it?"

"Sounds cool. Who'll we invite? The lunchtime gang? Bob and Lora Cornell? Cass Diedrich? Vonnie? Dick?"

Monique gave him a sidelong glance as she turned the corner at the school grounds. "Maybe we should forget about inviting anyone. Why not have a private show for just the two of us? I'd like that."

"Whatever you want," Randy said.

"Glady and Herman would be there to chaperon." She grinned at Randy and at the old-fashioned idea of a chaperon. Who would care what she did tonight?

"Where are your books?" Randy asked after Monique parked the Mercedes and thrust the keys into her shoulder purse.

"Books? What books?" Monique laughed. "I didn't take any home. I'll leave the greasy-grinding to you guys who're out for the Huntington scholarships."

"You should try for a scholarship, too, Monique. It'd give you a goal." Randy ran his fingers over the smooth leather of the seat upholstery.

"My goal is that diploma. And that's it. Once I've got that, my school days are behind me. I'll be my own person." She knew her parents wanted her to go on to college. Seven Sisters, of course. Smith. Wellesley. Or even Grinnell College somewhere on the vast unpeopled plains of Iowa. But she wasn't about to let herself in for more school days.

"What are your plans?"

"Don't ask hard questions so early in the morning." Monique brushed her silky hair over her shoulder in a practiced gesture, feeling it settle into a heavy fall against her back. "Plenty of time to make plans later." Plans. She tried to act flippant when anyone asked, but down deep she wished she had some plans. What did a person do when she got out of school? Work, she supposed. But what at? She couldn't think of any kind of work she wanted to do. Dad could probably get her on in the Tenneco offices, but she knew she'd hate that. File clerk. She'd never make megabucks at that. Filing's what people did who couldn't do anything else.

"The guys are really eyeballing this car," Randy said. "Look at that gang by the flagpole."

Monique was fully aware of the admiring glances the Mercedes rated from the guys passing by, and she enjoyed them. "Right, they are. But look. Here comes Dick Randall with an ornery gleam in his eye. He bugs me."

"Dick's okay," Randy said. "He just needs to grow up a little."

Dick patted a fender on the Mercedes then grabbed the front bumper and pretended to lift the car. Monique actually felt it move.

"Some show-off!" Monique said. "I don't know what Cass sees in that boy. She's a sharp girl. Why does she waste her time on Dick?"

"To each his own," Randy said. "I think Cass has been a good influence on Dick. He isn't quite as obnoxious with his jokes as he used to be."

"There's the first bell," Monique said. "We'd better go to our cages."

"Let's check the bulletin board," Randy said, once they had joined the throng of students filing through the back entry. "Might be some new announcements."

"Probably nothing good." Monique wrinkled her nose at the smell of chalk dust and sweeping compound, and she walked close to Randy as they approached the board.

"Hey! A new poster." Randy pointed. "Someone's starting a club."

"Graphology? That's the stuff about handwriting, isn't it? Sounds phony to me." She studied the red-and-white poster more carefully when she noticed that Randy seemed absorbed by it.

GRAPHOLOGY UNLIMITED!

JOIN NOW

Learn to analyze handwriting!
(Yours or someone else's)
What secrets does your handwriting hold? Find out at the first organizational meeting of GRAPHOLOGY UNLIMITED at Vonnie Morrison's house, 1515 Piney Glen, Tuesday, 7:00 p.m.

OPEN TO ALL STUDENTS
Please sign below.

"You aren't really interested are you, Randy?" Monique ignored the sign-up sheet.

"I think graphology's for real," he said.

"I'm surprised the school's sponsoring it. It has nothing to do with the curriculum. It's just a lot of speculation—fortune telling, actually. I can do the same thing with a deck of cards."

"The group's meeting at Vonnie's house." Randy ignored Monique's words as he ran a forefinger under the words. "Tomorrow night at seven. I've got nothing going on then. How about you?"

"Randy!" She thrust her lower lip into a pout. "You don't mean you're actually willing to waste a perfectly good night on a bunch of kids who're trying to play games with handwriting!"

"It's not just game playing," Randy said. "Vonnie really knows what she's talking about. She analyzed handwriting at a carnival booth back in September. Lots of kids were interested. Teachers, too."

"And you among them, I suppose."

"Well, yes, I was. I thought I'd let Vonnie take a look at my writing and see what she could make of it."

"What did she make of it?" Monique demanded. "I suppose she loaded on the flattery."

"Oh, she said..." Randy hesitated. "Well, I can't remember exactly what she said."

"Try harder."

"Well, she said my writing showed that I knew how to get along with people and that I had lots of energy."

"I suppose the whole student body crowded around, eager to pay a buck for a bit of ego building." Monique turned from the bulletin board, but she secretly wondered just what Vonnie Morrison would find to say about her own handwriting. Could she really pinpoint personality traits? Did handwriting really reveal the inner self? It might be worth attending just one club meeting to find out. Over and out. She wouldn't have to sign up for long-term membership.

"Vonnie doesn't hand out flattery," Randy said. "She actually tells you what traits she sees in your writing. If they're good, she tells you, of course. If they're not so good, she tells you that, too."

"That must make her a lot of enemies."

"Not so. She has a way about her. She doesn't hurt feelings."

The ruffle on Monique's blouse tickled her chin, reminding her of her dreary outfit. "Vonnie this. Vonnie that. I really get tired of hearing about Vonnie Morrison." She wanted to tell Randy she thought Vonnie was faking the diabetes scene just to get attention, but she didn't quite have the nerve to say that. It would make her sound jealous and petty. And she might be wrong. But she didn't think so. She had seen Vonnie in action at a party before the big shoplifting fiasco. When the going got rough for sweet little Vonnie, she copped out by staging an insulin reaction. Monique felt sure of it.

"You just need to get better acquainted with Vonnie," Randy said. "Let's sign up for the meeting. It'll be a blast. The whole gang will probably be there. Let's go for it."

"Color me absent. No way." She pouted again then laid her hand on the soft wool of his sweater sleeve. "If you want to spend an evening of boredom, that's your business. But frankly, I have better things to do with my time."

"Oh, come on, Monique. Be a sport. Vonnie'll need our support to get the group off the ground. We can go to the meeting then hang out at the pizzeria afterward. How about it?"

"Negative. You can sign up if you want to, but count me out." She watched, irritated, while Randy scribbled his name on the yellow sheet attached to the poster. What was she going to do? Maybe Randy actually wanted to be going out with Vonnie instead of with her. Maybe he was sorry she had returned from France. For sure, he hadn't had a case of the lonesomes while she was away.

"Maybe you'll change your mind before tomorrow," Randy said. "Think about it, okay?"

"Okay." She linked her arm through Randy's as they walked on toward the senior lockers. Maybe she should whisper a few words about Vonnie's phony diabetes to the girls in the rest room. Lots of rumors got started that way. Even if the rumors were false, they would give Vonnie a bad time for a while. She deserved it.

As soon as she had her books for morning classes, Monique went to first period English where she sat beside Tish Ewer. English. Dullsville. She wondered if Tish thought so, too. Before they could say anything to each other, Miss Baller scraped her chair back and stood. When she cleared her throat, the class came to attention. Miss Baller was a petite redhead who always wore long skirts and turned-up collars to make herself appear taller. She also had a low throaty voice that made everyone pay attention when she spoke.

"Students, I'm pleased to announce that the play books arrived during the weekend and that we'll have play tryouts tomorrow afternoon after school right in this room."

"What's the play?" someone called out.

"The name of it is *City Symphony*. As you might guess, the setting is a large American city. It calls for a cast of ten, and then, of course, we'll need behind-the-scenes workers. Makeup people. Props people. Lighting experts. Set designers. Prompters. Understudies. But tomorrow afternoon I want to see everybody who would like to try for a speaking part. We'll assign backstage duties later."

"Do we get to study the play books ahead of time?" Tish asked.

"No. Everyone will be reading parts for the first time. That's only fair."

"Can we choose the part we want to read?" Monique asked.

"Yes," Miss Baller said. "When you arrive tomorrow afternoon I'll give everyone a brief synopsis of the plot, then you can read any part you choose. I'll be the final judge of which part you get, however, and it just might be one you didn't actually try for."

"That could be a drag," Monique whispered to Tish.

Tish started to reply, but Miss Baller had already begun the day's lecture. Monique's mind wandered immediately. *City Symphony.* The title sounded sophisticated. She wondered about the characters. Surely they would be sophisticated, too. Being in a play might be fun. She imagined herself on center stage under a spotlight that emphasized her high cheekbones, the planes of her face.

The minute the dismissal bell rang, Monique spoke to Tish. "Let's try out, Tish. It might be cool. You ever been in a play?"

"No." Tish raised her voice above the sound of pounding feet and slamming locker doors. "But I'll try out if you will. Just think. Us on stage and the whole school watching. Neat, right?"

"Right." Then Monique's shoulders slumped.

"What's wrong?"

"I can't report here after school and neither can you. At least I assume you're still working at the library."

"Yuck! I forgot." Tish sighed.

"Maybe we could get our hours changed," Monique suggested. "After all, the play's a school project. Maybe we could trade working hours with someone who's scheduled on Saturday."

"Let's call Mr. Gomez at the library tomorrow during lunch hour," Tish said. "He's out of town today, remember? How many more hours do you have to work?"

Monique figured rapidly in her head. The security officer at Neiman-Marcus had assigned her forty hours of community service work as part of her punishment for the shoplifting incident, and although it seemed as if she had been working forever, she still had megahours to go.

"How many?" Tish asked.

"Thirty-two," Monique admitted, pausing for breath at the top of the stairs. "When you just do two a day, it takes a long time."

"Like sixteen days," Tish said. "Even I can figure that out."

"Maybe I could work all of Saturday. Eight whole hours." She clicked her ball-point eight times for emphasis. "Two Saturdays—two miserable Saturdays and I'd be a free person again."

"But I won't," Tish said. "I'm working for the money, remember? I may not be able to juggle my work hours around a bunch of play practices."

"We can ask," Monique said. "The worst Mr. Gomez can say is no."

Monique spent the rest of the morning imagining herself on center stage with Randy and Vonnie and the whole student body watching her, hanging on to her every word. Just before noon she and Tish met at their lockers.

"Let's meet the gang for lunch as usual," Monique said. "Don't say anything about the play today. Then tomorrow—tomorrow we can dramatically excuse ourselves from the lunch table to make the call."

"Good deal." Tish leaned toward Monique and began whispering. "Let's be very secretive about our plans. Make the gang wonder what we're up to. We'll be women of mystery."

Monique followed Tish as they hurried down the hall. She had watched Tish in action as she vied with Vonnie for Bob's attention. Maybe Tish would be her friend. They had three things in common. They both worked at the library, they both wanted to be in the play and they both disliked Vonnie Morrison.

Two

On Tuesday Vonnie hardly noticed the prick of the needle as she gave herself her insulin shot. Once she was dressed, she slipped on her silver medical bracelet and went to the kitchen.

"Wish I could skip breakfast," she said, trying to ignore the faint turpentine odor that clung to her mother's painting smock. "It's the pits having to eat when I'm not hungry, especially today when I'm up up up about the graphology club."

"I know how you must feel," her mother said. "But no skipping meals."

"Right." Vonnie poured their milk and juice while her mother fixed some cereal and toast. Diabetics didn't skip meals. She had learned that lesson the hard way, but that was all behind her now. She didn't intend to have any more insulin reactions because of her own disobedience or carelessness.

"Still planning that one-woman show?" Vonnie asked.

"Right. And I need a few more landscapes to balance the still lifes and the portraits."

Her mother wanted to have the show soon. She had been painting like crazy ever since they had moved to Houston, and Vonnie knew her painting helped make up for a lack of friends. Their frequent moves were hard on her parents as well as herself.

"Mom, what if nobody wants to join the graphology club? That'd be some put-down."

"Relax, Vonnie. You'll have some takers. You'll see. The kids were begging you to start the group, weren't they?"

"Well, yes, but ..."

"They'll be here. Relax."

"I hope you're right." Vonnie finished eating quickly, and dashed from the house into the cool morning. She did a double take when she saw Bob at the wheel of his family's car and Lora sitting in the back seat with the posters they had made the night before. Usually she and Lora walked to school alone.

"Thought you two needed a ride this morning," Bob said. "Did I rush you?"

"No. I was ready. But what about your computer club?"

"I'll be a few minutes late today. No big deal. I'll just tell the others I was in a slow mode."

"Thanks a bunch." Vonnie knew how much the computer club meant to Bob, and she felt flattered that he had given up some minutes of it to help her and Lora with the graphology posters.

After the short drive to school, Bob parked in the student lot and they carried the posters inside. "You got plenty of thumbtacks?"

"Right." Vonnie picked up two posters, leaving the other two for Lora. When they reached the bulletin board, they were dismayed to find it already full of announcement sheets.

"Now what?" Vonnie shook the box of thumbtacks, listening to their rattle. "I'm glad we got the two big posters up yesterday morning."

"We'll take some of this old stuff down," Lora said. "No sweat. Lots of it's outdated."

They crumpled old announcements, rearranging the others until they had space for their poster.

"What color?" Lora asked.

"The red-and-white one," Vonnie said. "It's a grabber."

After tacking the notice in place, they went to another board, placing a yellow poster there. They were just inserting the last tack when they heard heels clicking along the hallway.

"What are you doing, girls?" Miss Hunt asked.

"Placing an announcement." Vonnie stood aside as Miss Hunt studied the poster carefully.

"Who's the leader of this group? You, Vonnie?"

"Yes."

"I'd like to talk to you about this," Miss Hunt said.

"All right." Vonnie waited, feeling she should say more, yet her mind went totally blank.

"I have a meeting right now. Could you come to the journalism room after school?"

Vonnie hesitated. The afternoon right before the meeting! She had planned to get home early to see that everything was in order for the guests, but she was curious.

"Okay. I'll be there." Vonnie pretended to adjust the poster as she and Lora waited for Miss Hunt to leave.

"What do you suppose she wants?" Lora said when the woman was out of earshot.

"I can't imagine. I haven't got her for any classes."

"Me either. And speaking of classes—there's the bell."

"Yeah. We'd better get going."

The morning passed quickly, and as Vonnie and her friends gathered in their usual corner of the lunchroom, Vonnie realized that most of them had seen the graphology posters on the bulletin boards. Between garlic-laced bites of spaghetti and meatballs they wanted to know more about the club.

"How many have signed up?" Bob sat by Vonnie as he frequently did, but almost before they were seated, Tish Ewer joined the group, sitting directly across from them and managing to give Bob her undivided attention.

"I counted seven names," Tish said, frowning slightly as Lora sat beside her and began talking, distracting her from Bob.

The scent of gardenia wafted in the air as Monique flung her long blond hair over her shoulder, narrowly missing Randy's dish of sliced peaches. "A graphology club? You've got to be kidding. Who'd be interested in such a faddy club?"

"Graphology's no fad, Monique." Vonnie's throat tightened. She wasn't about to let Monique bad-mouth the club. "It's recognized as a science by many business and professional people."

"Maybe by pixies, elves and leprechauns." Monique laughed.

"My dad uses it every day in his personnel work for Eckert Electronics," Vonnie said.

"You can't look at my writing and tell me anything about myself that I don't already know," Monique insisted.

"Maybe not." Vonnie took a sip of cool milk before she spoke again, determined not to let Monique get to her. "But some people are surprised at what their handwriting reveals."

"It knocks their socks off," Lora said.

"I was impressed when Vonnie analyzed my writing at the school carnival." Randy stretched his long legs under the table and drank half a carton of milk with only two sips on the straw.

"What did she tell you?" Monique put her hand on his arm. "Give, Randy. It had to be more than that wimpy stuff about energy. Are you keeping secrets from me?"

Randy's face flushed. "I forget exactly what Vonnie told me, but at the time it showed me some new insights."

"He's just being modest," Vonnie said.

"I suppose you remember his writing quite clearly," Monique said.

"Bet she remembers mine, too." Dick Randall laughed so hard that kids at other tables turned to stare. "She said I might die from terminal overexposure."

"Dick!" Vonnie said. "Get real. That's not what I said. I said that your writing indicated you were awesomely outgoing."

"You're an extrovert, Dick," Cass said. "There's nothing wrong with being an extrovert."

"I'm interested in Randy's writing," Monique said. "Not yours, Dick."

"Pardon me for living." Dick slurped a strand of spaghetti, which left a trail of meat sauce on his chin.

"Give, Vonnie," Monique ordered. "What did Randy's writing show?"

"He's already told you his script showed that he used a great deal of pressure on the pen," Vonnie said. "To a graphologist that indicates the writer has lots of energy."

"Most football players do," Monique said. "Class presidents, too." She patted Randy's arm. "So what else is new? That doesn't reveal anything I didn't already know."

"Don't tell her anything else," Lora said. "Make her come to the meeting if she wants to know more."

"I wouldn't waste my time on your silly meeting." Monique gave her full attention to her spaghetti as if it were a gourmet treat straight from Paris.

"You can bet I'll be there," Cass Diedrich said. "I thought handwriting analysis was a lot of bunk until Vonnie talked about mine. 'Outgoing, but thoughtful.' It's the truth. You can't blame me for wanting to hear more. I'll be at the meeting and Dick's coming with me, aren't you, Dick?"

"Guess so—if you say so." Dick ran his hand over his bristly Mohawk haircut as he smiled at Cass.

"What's it mean when your writing slants uphill?" Bob asked. "Sometimes my writing looks like the side of a mountain."

"That shows that you're an optimist who likes what you're doing or what you're writing about," Vonnie said.

"What were you writing about?" Tish Ewer clattered her fork onto her tray and gave Bob her full attention.

"It was an English theme on the user-friendly aspects of computers as word processors," Bob said. "Got an A on it, too."

"That figures," Tish said. "Optimism. Enthusiasm. That's the real you where computers are concerned."

"I suppose if the writing slants downhill, that means terminal pessimism." Dick leaned back in his chair until the two rear legs squeaked a protest.

"It could," Vonnie agreed.

"That's the way mine goes," Dick said. "Especially on history tests."

"Terminal. Terminal." Cass scowled at Dick. "Is that your new word for the week? I think I'm going to die from terminal boredom at hearing you use the word terminal!"

"What's it mean when a person dots *i*'s with tiny round circles instead of regular dots?" Monique asked.

"Don't tell her," Lora said.

Vonnie hesitated, feeling as if she were on a roller coaster poised for the plunge. A too positive answer might encourage Monique to attend the meeting, and she really didn't want her there. But if she sounded too negative, Monique might stay away and influence others to do the same. She couldn't risk that.

"Circles instead of dots are common in the handwriting of young people and artistically talented people," Vonnie said. Mentally she congratulated herself for saying "young" instead of immature and "artistically talented" instead of "show-offy." A graphologist also had to be a diplomat.

"And what if the writer draws smiling faces inside the circles?" Monique asked.

"The same thing, only more so," Lora said before Vonnie could reply. "At least that'd be my guess."

"Right," Vonnie agreed. "Many times graphology is a matter of using common sense."

"Does your mother dot her *i*'s with circles?" Bob asked Vonnie. "She's artistically talented."

"No, but her writing shows lots of other flourishes." Vonnie crunched a piece of celery. A few minutes ago she had been starving, yet now she hardly felt hungry at all. She shouldn't let Monique get to her this way. Her hands and the back of her neck felt cold—for her a certain sign of nerves. She wished Monique would stay out of her space.

"I'm not sure I want everyone learning about the inner workings of *my* personality," Tish said. "I mean, it's...like very revealing."

"I don't think Vonnie's revelations will tarnish your image in the eyes of the whole solar system," Lora said, making no attempt to hide her sarcasm.

"I definitely agree with Tish," Monique said. "Is the world going to be richer if all our miseries are shared?"

"Who mentioned miseries?" Lora asked. "What we'll have here is your basic group of interested and friendly kids. We'll be working together to know one another better."

"To psych each other out, you mean," Dick said.

"It's not as if Vonnie's going to spit out the private details of our characters on *Good Morning, America*," Lora said.

"Right," Randy agreed. "Lora's got it. It'll be a club for the privileged view. Pun intended. I plan to be there."

"Randy!" Monique said, pouting prettily. "You're kidding."

"No, I'm not. I think it's going to be a fun group. Vonnie needs our support, so let's give it to her."

"How often will the club meet?" Tish asked.

"I'd like it to meet every other week at first," Vonnie said.

"Count me out," Monique said. "The whole idea's V.D."

"V.D.?" Lora asked, breaking the sudden silence that followed Monique's comment.

Vonnie felt her face flush in anger rather than in embarrassment. Hot face. Cold hands and neck. Maybe she needed a piece of candy.

"V.D.," Monique repeated in her look-at-me voice. "Very dumb. That's what I think of graphology." Monique picked up her tray and swished her shimmery hair. "Come on, Tish. We've got an important phone call to make."

"Right." Tish picked up her tray and trailed after Monique.

Lora's gaze followed the two girls across the cafeteria. "What you have there are two basic nerds. Give 'em the deep six, Vonnie. We'll all be at the meeting to back you up.

And listen, gang." Lora paused until she had everyone's attention. "Let's each of us bring a friend who isn't at this table."

"Agreed," Bob said. "Everyone bring one."

As lunch ended and they filed back to their classes, Vonnie talked privately with Lora. "You think Rod will be there?"

"He said he would, but who knows?"

"You should know, that's who."

"We're not going steady anymore. We have an understanding."

Vonnie welcomed that news. She and Lora had been best friends until Lora dumped her in favor of Rod. It had hurt, but she had recovered. Last month Lora had been convinced she wanted nothing in her future but home and family. It had taken Vonnie, Bob and Lora's parents to convince her that she needed to give herself more options. Maybe Monique had influenced her, too. The near arrest for shoplifting had made the whole gang think more carefully about the future and what it might hold for them.

Best friends. How she missed Hannah back in Kansas. Maybe she had leaped too quickly into her friendship with Lora. They would always be friends, but not best friends. She missed having someone she could share her inner feelings with. Cass was too involved with Dick to listen to anyone else. She and Tish got along, but just barely. And sharing thoughts with Monique was totally out of the question.

Vonnie pulled her thoughts back to the present. "Is Rod going out with someone else?"

"I don't really know. Maybe. He's working more and more gigs with Roy Cooper's band. At least that's where he says he spends his Saturday nights."

"Then that's where he probably spends them. No reason he'd do a number on you. He's as gone on music as Bob is on computers."

"Good deal," Lora said. "It keeps them off the streets. But Rod did say he'd attend the graphology meeting."

Vonnie hoped the kids would follow Lora's suggestion to bring a friend to the meeting. What if Monique talked Randy out of attending? Vonnie felt Dick would be there only to please Cass. The meeting could flop.

After classes that afternoon, Vonnie hurried to the journalism room. Three kids were ahead of her, and all three were waiting to see Miss Hunt who was busy going over advertising layouts for the back page of *The Iconoclast*. Vonnie sat down in a back seat, feeling caught up in the hustle-bustle of the room as more students came and went.

She recognized Scott Monroe, the sports editor, and Candy Johnson, a roving reporter. Randy came in, leaving a page of senior class notes on Miss Hunt's desk. The room pulsed with excitement, and Vonnie wondered what it would be like to be a working part of it. But she wasn't a part of it. After fifteen minutes she stood. Miss Hunt was so busy that she had probably forgotten she had asked Vonnie to stop by. Vonnie headed toward the door, hoping Lora might have waited for her.

"Vonnie," Miss Hunt called. "Just a minute, please."

Vonnie turned toward Miss Hunt's desk, sitting right in the front row. Three more students brought short articles for Miss Hunt's inspection before she gave Vonnie her full attention.

"Thanks for waiting, Vonnie." Miss Hunt tucked a yellow pencil behind her right ear. "I want to talk to you about that graphology group you're starting. How about writing an article on it for the school paper?"

Vonnie's mouth suddenly went so dry that she could hardly swallow. She dropped her pencil, then picked it up, using that brief time span to get her bearings.

"How long would the article have to be?"

"Six hundred words would make a nice column, or a thousand to twelve hundred words would make a feature article. I'll let you take your choice. Will you try it?"

"How soon do you have to have it?"

"The next deadline is a week from Wednesday afternoon. Can you make that?"

"I think so. I'm not a fast writer, but . . ."

"The paper will come out the Friday following the Wednesday deadline. Can I count on you for an article?"

"I'll think about it and let you know," Vonnie said. "And thanks for asking me. Writing for the paper sounds like fun."

Vonnie left the journalism room quickly and was surprised to find Randy waiting for her in the hall.

"What gives?" Randy asked. "You writing for *The Iconoclast*?"

"Maybe. Nothing definite about it yet."

"You look ready to crash. Want a ride home?"

"That'd be neat. I'm in sort of a hurry, but where's Monique?"

"Play practice. If you'll remember, she and Tish were acting very mysterious at lunch. That's what it was all about. She and Tish disappeared into the English room together right after the bell rang. Let's split."

"Lora may be waiting for me out front."

"Negative. I saw her leave with Rod ten minutes ago."

"Let's check the sign-up sheets on the bulletin boards," Vonnie said. "I'd like to know how many kids to expect tonight."

"Right." Randy headed toward the board at the side entry. "Not a lot going here. One name."

"Who?"

"Dick Randall." Randy laughed. "Bet Cass signed on the board by the front door and Dick signed here to fool her into thinking he isn't going to attend."

"That figures." They walked to the other side entry board where there were no names. Vonnie felt her hopes drop to her toes. What if nobody came but kooky Dick Randall!

But at the front board the news was better. She read the list. "Bob. Lora. Cass. Randy. Rod. Candy. Monique." She turned the Randy. "I see you talked Monique into coming."

"Yeah. It was easy. Just took a little persuasion."

A little persuasion. Vonnie thought about that. She knew from the lunchroom conversation that Monique had been dead set against attending the meeting. Either she was afraid to let Randy attend without her, or she was coming with the express intent of causing trouble. Maybe both reasons were correct. One could expect almost anything where Monique was concerned.

"I see Tish Ewer has signed up, too." Randy ran his forefinger under Tish's name. "Think she's more interested in Bob than she is in handwriting."

"Who knows!" Vonnie tried to act unconcerned, but she couldn't help the feeling of dismay that washed over her at the sight of Tish's name. Did she have to follow Bob everywhere!

"See! Dick's name isn't here." Randy laughed. "Bet he has Cass in a snit."

"Cass should be on to his ways by now. I'm worried that he'll try to fake me out with his writing. I'm sure he'll try to disguise it in a way that'll make me say something stupid."

"Don't call on him," Randy said. "Work with other samples. Banish him to the minor leagues for the evening."

"I can't ignore him forever. But maybe I could get by with it for the first meeting."

Randy drove Vonnie home quickly, and she half hoped Monique would see them together. It would serve her right for acting as if she owned Randy.

"Thanks a bunch, Randy," Vonnie said as she slammed the car door. "See you tonight."

"I'm looking forward to it, Von."

As Randy revved the motor and drove on down the street, Vonnie looked after him with a feeling of envy. Randy knew where he was going. College. Business major. In fact most of the seniors seemed to have more direction to their lives than she did. Bob was going into computer work. Lora had decided to go to college and she was thinking of a home ec major. But what about herself? She wished she had an important goal.

But now was no time to be setting long-range goals. She needed to face the short-term deadline of the graphology meeting. Hurrying inside, she began making last-minute preparations. What if the meeting bombed?

Three

On Tuesday, as planned, Monique led the way from the lunchroom, threading her way slowly and carefully between tables, fighting an urge to look over her shoulder to see if Randy and the rest of the gang were watching her. She could imagine what they were saying and thinking. *Why are those two leaving in such a big hurry to make a phone call? Who are they going to call? And what about? They're up to something.* A delicious shiver feathered up her spine.

Tish dropped her notebook and that gave them both an excuse to stop, gather up the scattered papers and glance back at their friends without their curiosity being noticed.

"They're watching," Monique said, once more turning her back on her friends. "Vonnie and Lora are whispering and looking at us, and they're both frowning."

"Naturally." Tish rearranged her books, held her head high and followed Monique into the hall. "See? We're already actresses. We're making a dramatic exit from stage left and holding our audience spellbound."

Monique knew she was an actress without Tish telling her. Anyone who could wear a suit with a French "Mimi" label and a brown shirt with silk collar and cuffs to school without wearing a bag over her head to hide her identity was giving a performance that deserved an Oscar.

"You got a quarter?" Monique asked, forgetting her audience for the moment as she considered more practical concerns.

Tish opened her shoulder bag and pulled out her billfold. "You so out of bread you don't even have a quarter? Your dad really must have you on a short string."

"I've got to pay off that debt at Neiman's. If I carry money with me, I spend it. If I don't carry it with me, then I can't spend it. It's that simple. I've got this humongous lack of willpower."

"I know how it is," Tish said. "Sometimes it takes most of my allowance to buy the books and floppy disks I need to keep Bob convinced I'm deeply into computers. But I've got a quarter."

"I'll pay you back."

"We'll split the cost." Tish pretended to think. "Twelve and a half cents each."

Tish giggled, but Monique thought it gross to be in a position that required discussing the cost of a phone call. Haggling over pennies would never be her big thing.

"I'll look up the number." Monique lifted the bulky directory hanging from a chain beneath the phone.

"Don't bother," Tish said. "I've got it memorized, I've dialed it so many times."

Monique held her ear near the receiver and heard the phone ring three times before the desk clerk answered.

"This is Tish Ewer. May I speak to Mr. Gomez, please?"

"One moment. Will you hold?"

"Yes."

They waited.

"What if he says no?" Monique asked.

"Then we go to work as usual. What else!"

But once Mr. Gomez came on the line and heard Tish's plea, he granted permission for them to attend play practice and work on Saturday afternoon. Tish replaced the receiver and they grinned at each other triumphantly.

"Maybe we shouldn't have told him exactly why we wanted to make the change," Monique said.

"Why not?"

"If we don't get parts in the play, we'll look like wimps. Sometimes there's no point in telling the whole world your business. Glady, our housekeeper, calls it keeping one's own counsel."

"And you lap up advice from the housekeeper?"

"From Glady, I do. And from Herman, too—sometimes, that is. But Glady's more than just a housekeeper, Tish. She's my friend. She listens to me."

"Poor little rich girl with nobody to understand her. You're breaking my heart."

"Come off it, Tish."

"You come off it. Telling Mr. Gomez our plans was hardly informing the whole world. Next time I'll get your permission before I speak. Or better yet, bring your own quarter and you can make your own call."

"Oh, come on Tish. I wasn't criticizing."

"You could have fooled me."

"Tish..." Monique hesitated. How had they gotten into an argument? And really over nothing important. If she wanted Tish for a friend, she was going to have to be more careful about offending her. She gulped. "Tish, I'm sorry. You did a great job talking to Mr. Gomez. It doesn't matter that he knows about play tryouts. You got us exactly what we wanted.''

"You're right. I did." They walked toward the history room, half expecting the bell to ring. When it didn't, Tish leaned against the wall beside the door, bracing one foot behind her and balancing on the other leg like a stork. "Monique, what do you think of this group Vonnie's trying to organize?''

Monique hugged her books in front of her as if they were a shield. "I think just what I said during lunch. It's V.D. Very dumb.''

"But are you going to sign up? How can you walk away from it? I mean, if Randy attends the meeting, you'll want to be sure to be there, too, won't you?''

"You hint that I'm jealous of Vonnie, and you're past history." Monique spat the words then wished she could yank them back. She and Tish were close to arguing again.

"I wasn't hinting at anything, Monique. I just know how I feel about Bob. I hate seeing him around Vonnie. I thought you might feel the same way about Vonnie and Randy.''

"Whatever was between those two is old news," Monique said. "But I've got an idea.''

"Give.''

"Let's both sign the attendance sheet for the meeting. It'll please the guys.''

"It may please Randy, but I'm not sure Bob cares whether or not I sign up.''

"Well, our signatures on the sheet will give Vonnie something to think about. They might punch a couple of holes in her self-assurance.''

"You really don't like her, do you?''

"Read my lips! N-O.''

"Okay, so you dislike her.''

"And you?'' Monique countered.

"I might like her okay if she weren't going out with Bob. She's really sort of fun and she has neat ideas. But . . ."

"But she's going out with Bob, right?"

"Right. She definitely is. They may not be card-carrying steadies, but they could fool the world."

"Let's go sign the sheet." Monique grabbed Tish's wrist, almost pulling her off balance as she tugged her along toward the bulletin board. "Scare tactics. Our signatures will worry Vonnie, and Randy'll think he persuaded me to sign because he did. We can decide later whether or not we'll actually attend the meeting."

Before they'd finished signing the attendance sheet, the bell rang and they headed for afternoon classes. Monique thought the day would never end. A fly buzzed endlessly against the windowpane. The electric clock clicked, and the long hand jerked forward as it slowly marked the minutes. Play tryouts. Who cared about history and math and English? Maybe she could be an actress. Now that would be a glamorous job that she'd like. Why hadn't she thought of it before? Acting. There were probably lots of schools that had courses in acting. Maybe even Ivy League schools that would please her parents. "Monique Wagar?"

Monique heard her name like an echo from a great distance, then suddenly she realized the teacher and the whole class were looking at her. And waiting.

"I'm sorry, Miss Hoover. I was thinking of something else and I didn't hear what you said."

"That's quite obvious." The teacher held Monique's full attention with her determined gaze. "I asked you to name one outstanding leader of Union forces."

Monique felt her face flush. What did she know about unions. Her family was definitely antiunion. She prodded her memory, dredging up a name she had heard her father mention many times during the past years. "Do you mean a union leader like Jimmy Hoffa?"

Her face flushed even hotter when the class tittered. Miss Hoover snapped her history text shut and frowned as she paced the narrow area in the front of the classroom.

"Monique, did you read any of the history assignment for today?"

"Well, not exactly. You see...that is, last night I had all this other work to do and..."

"I understand," Miss Hoover said. "Monique, we're studying about the Civil War, not about labor problems. For tomorrow I want you to write a paper listing Union leaders and Confederate leaders along with brief sentences about each man and the battles in which he was involved."

"Yes, ma'am." Relief washed through her as Miss Hoover called on someone else to recite, and the class settled down again. Union. Confederate. Who cared? She cared. At least she cared about having to write that extra paper. Maybe Glady would give her a crash course on the Civil War.

When the bell finally rang, Monique hurried to her locker so intent on play tryouts that she forgot about meeting Randy.

"Ready to go the library?" he asked.

"Big news!" Monique smiled brightly, hoping Randy had been wondering about her mysterious lunchtime behavior all afternoon. "Tish Ewer and I are trying out for the play. We got our afternoon library hours changed—for today at least. Why don't you come to tryouts?" She took his hand, pulling him toward the English room. "You might get a part."

"No way." Randy stood firm. "Acting isn't my thing."

"Have you ever tried it?" She tilted her head to one side, letting her hair fall against his arm.

"No."

"Then how can you be so sure it isn't your thing?"

"I'm sure. Believe me, I'm sure. I couldn't get up in front of people and act like some other character. Being Randy Morrison is all I can handle."

"Randy Morrison's just fine with me." Monique gave him a warm smile as she linked her arm through his.

"How about attending the graphology meeting tonight?" Randy asked.

"You've got it. I've already signed up." She gave his arm a squeeze. "You talked me into it, after all."

"Great! I'll pick up a little before seven. Is that a deal?"

"I'll be ready." They walked toward the English room together, pausing at the door. Laughter rang from within the room, but Monique thought it sounded like nervous laughter. "Wish me luck, Randy. I'm really excited about getting a part in that play. It could make school a lot less of a drag."

"Luck!" Randy squeezed her hand. "I'll see you tonight."

Monique hurried into the English room, spotted Tish and took a seat right behind her. A play book lay on each desk, and Monique picked hers up, smelling the fresh-ink scent as she started looking through it.

"Okay, kids," Miss Baller said. "I'm glad to see so many of you here this afternoon. I'll tell you what we're going to do. First, I'll need a couple of you boys to push my desk to one side so we'll have a small stage area up front."

Four boys rushed forward, scraping the desk across the floorboards and leaving scratch marks behind. Then Miss Baller spoke again.

"Briefly, the play concerns two girls who've moved to the city from small towns and who are hunting jobs. They're roommates. They both have boyfriends who are employed. The plot revolves on their adventures and misadventures in the city, and the theme is one of perseverance leading to success.''

That was Miss Baller for you, Monique thought. Always analyzing a story to death, probing for motivations and themes and character traits. But she listened attentively.

"Now," Miss Baller continued. "You're going to take turns reading the parts. The first scene opens with two characters on stage speaking to each other, then two more enter from stage left and join in the conversation."

"Do we have to go through the actions, too?" someone asked.

"I want you to stand on the make-shift stage," Miss Baller said. "If you can coordinate some actions with the words, fine. But I won't expect that. Just read the words with feeling. Who'll be first? I need two girls and two boys."

Monique poked Tish and whispered, "Hang tight. Let someone else be first."

When nobody volunteered, Miss Baller selected four people, and Monique breathed easier when she realized neither she nor Tish had been called. The four on stage read through the words stiffly and tentatively. Monique knew she could do better than that. And she wouldn't be too nervous to move around if the part called for it. She wasn't so dumb that she couldn't breathe and think at the same time.

"Fine, kids," Miss Baller said when the first group finished. "Any volunteers for the second reading?"

This time Monique poked Tish and they both raised their hands.

"Monique. Tish. Fine. Now let's have two boys." She waited and when no hands went up she appointed two. "Ryan. Jason. You're on."

Monique chose the part of the outgoing popular girl while Tish read the lines of the shy girl. Perfect. The parts were made for them. Monique managed movements and gestures at the same time she used voice inflections that suited the lines.

"Very well done," Miss Baller said when they finished. "Now who'll be next?"

"Will you make your choices today?" Monique asked.

"Yes. As soon as everyone's had a chance to try out, I'll give you my decisions. If you can't wait, you'll find the names posted on the bulletin board tomorrow morning."

"We've got to wait," Monique whispered to Tish.

"Right. We do. I want to see how the rest of the kids do. I think we were good, don't you?"

Monique winked. Then they watched four more groups go through the lines. After everyone had tried out, Miss Baller consulted her notes and wrote in a large notebook. The room was so quiet that Monique could hear the pencil scratching across the page.

"Okay, kids. I want to thank every one of you for reading this afternoon. If you didn't get a part, don't be discouraged. There'll be another play in a few months and you can try again. Also, any of you who didn't get a part will be welcome to help backstage. Watch the bulletin boards for announcements concerning rehearsals."

"Who gets the parts?" someone asked.

"Here's the cast." Miss Baller began reading names, but Monique heard nothing after she heard her name and Tish's name and realized they had been chosen.

"We made it, Tish!" she said after Miss Baller had finished and the cast members were congratulating each other. "We made it. We're in!"

"Oh, Monique! I'm so glad we tried out. Being in the play's going to be a gas!" They were gathering their things in preparation of leaving when Miss Baller spoke again.

"Cast members, attention. The first play practice will be tonight. Meet in the auditorium promptly at seven o'clock.

I'll expect everyone to be there. If you can't be present, let me know now. The success of a play depends on well-attended rehearsals.''

"Great," Monique said once they were outside and on their way to Tish's old Ford. "Now we'll have good reason to skip the graphology meeting tonight."

"I sort of wanted to go to it," Tish said. "I hate just sitting back and letting Vonnie monopolize Bob."

"I don't call getting a part in the play and going to play practice sitting back. Maybe you'll meet a new guy in the play cast. Someone you'll really fall for." Monique reached over and honked the horn just for the fun of it. "Hey, Houston, You've got two new actresses in town!"

"Maybe there'll be some new guys to consider," Tish said. "But I'm not counting on it. They've all probably got steadies who won't let them out of their sight."

"Maybe you could get Bob to volunteer as a stagehand. That would be interesting."

"No way. He's too deeply into computers to give any free time to the drama department."

As soon as Monique got home from school, she telephoned Randy with the good news about the play. "Randy, I wish you had tried out for a part. We could have had lots of fun together in the cast."

"Maybe I'll volunteer as a stagehand."

"Neat!" Leaning toward the phone, she gripped the receiver more tightly. "That would be great. We're practicing tonight. Can you be there?"

"Hold it one little minute. I'm not volunteering for tonight. I'm going to the graphology meeting. I'll see you tomorrow."

"Or maybe you'll see me later tonight." She tried for a low whispery voice, counting on it to stir his curiosity.

"How? We can't be in two places at the same time."

"Randy, how about the one who's free first meeting the other? When we're together, we can go to the pizzeria and rap about the evening."

"Deal. If I finish first, I'll come to the school. If you finish first, you come to Vonnie's."

Monique couldn't remember when she had been so excited about anything that had to do with school. She had Glady bring her tossed salad and roast veal to her room on a tray so she could eat while she studied the play book.

Skim milk. Glady was trying to sneak her on a diet. Maybe it wasn't such a bad idea at that. She wanted to look her best on stage. Costumes! Would she have to furnish her own, or did the drama department have a store of sophisticated gowns? She had a million questions to ask Miss Baller tonight.

In less than an hour she had memorized five pages of her part. She surprised herself. Maybe she wasn't so dumb, after all. Maybe she just needed a strong incentive to learn, and maybe this play was that incentive!

Promptly at seven o'clock Miss Baller greeted the cast members at the auditorium door, snapping the lock after everyone was inside.

"Now, kids, we're going to get right to work. And we're going to hit it hard for an hour and a half. Then you're dismissed. You can count on that as our routine. Hard work. Prompt dismissal."

"How often will we practice?" Tish asked.

"Three nights a week." Miss Baller led the way to the stage. "Reserve Tuesday, Wednesday, Thursday for play practice for the next four weeks. That should bring us close to performance readiness, if all goes well. We may do some excerpts for an assembly before that. It's good to have some on-stage experience before the actual performance."

"Who's going to run the lights?" a boy asked.

"We'll just have general overhead lighting for now," Miss Baller said. "I'll work with backstage crews later in the week. Now I want to hear and see you run through the first act. If it goes well and there's time, we'll try the second act, too."

Miss Baller had chalk-marked the stage floor, indicating the furniture that would be present, showing where each character would stand. The rehearsal began.

Monique said her lines with feeling, moving freely about the stage from imaginary couch to imaginary chair while the others kept their gazes glued to the play books and moved awkwardly from place to place. After a few minutes Miss Baller stopped them.

"Hold it, kids. Monique. Step forward, please."

Monique stepped forward, putting a bright smile, but inwardly wondering what she had done wrong.

"Are you familiar with this play? Have you performed this part before?"

"No. I saw the play book for the first time this afternoon."

"But you aren't using your book."

"I memorized a few pages of it after you dismissed us." Again Monique felt her face flush, but this time it was a flush of pleasure. "I think I can have the whole first act memorized by the end of the week."

"Wonderful, Monique. I can see I've picked a winner. All right, cast, begin at the top of page four. Project your voices. Enunciate. Use your lips, your teeth, your tongue. Get those words across."

True to her promise, Miss Baller dismissed them exactly an hour and a half after they had arrived.

"Monique, you were great," Tish said once they were outside. "How did you memorize all those lines so quickly?"

"I don't know exactly." Monique wondered the same thing herself. "But it seemed easy. I just really got into my character's skin, I guess. I concentrated on the character and the words just stuck in my mind."

"You're a lot like your character," Tish said. "Beautiful. Outgoing. Always with a smooth retort no matter what's said to you."

"Are you saying I wasn't really acting?" Monique demanded, surprised at the edge she heard in her voice.

"No, of course not. I just meant..."

Monique let it pass. Why should she take offense at Tish's words? Tish had said she was beautiful, hadn't she? Tonight the whole world was a beautiful place.

"You going home now?" Tish asked.

"No. I'm going to Vonnie's. The graphology meeting, remember?"

"Sure I remember. But we've got a great excuse for not showing. Everyone'll think we're still at play practice."

Monique told Tish about her arrangement with Randy, and when Tish looked disappointed, Monique grinned. "Thought you wanted to see Bob tonight."

"Well, I did, but..."

"Then here's your chance. What better way to be noticed than to break into the graphology meeting midway through! The gang can hardly ignore us."

"True."

"I'm betting they'll be more interested in hearing about play practice than in learning more about handwriting. You could find yourself hanging out with Bob before the night's over."

"You may be right at that, Monique. Let's go. Sometimes Bob doesn't notice me at all if Vonnie's around, but I have a feeling he's going to notice me tonight."

"Right," Monique agreed. "Count on it. I'm going to breeze in there, collect Randy and take off for the bright lights. Vonnie'll be left in awesome shock, wondering what happened to her meeting."

Four

Vonnie spent the short time before the club meeting inspecting her living room and trying to see it as her guests would see it that evening. The tan carpeting and draperies blended with the off-white walls, offering a background suitable for almost anyone. The earth-toned couch and the russet easy chairs gave the room a restful atmosphere, and Vonnie appreciated that. She wanted this to be a relaxed evening.

After she set up a few extra folding chairs, she placed dishes of pink and green mints on two corner tables, knowing she might need some candy in a hurry if she began to feel faint. But that was negative thinking. She wasn't about to feel faint. She had never felt stronger and more in charge.

"How many kids are you expecting?" her mother asked. "Do you have enough chairs?"

"I'm not sure. Ten had signed up when I left school, and some of them may bring friends. But don't worry. If there's an overflow, we can sit on the floor."

"Do you have plenty of paper and pencils?" Her mother laid a clipboard on the card table Vonnie had set up at one end of the room.

"Everything's ready, Mom. Relax. Can we have an early dinner?"

"It's in the oven. Chicken casserole. We'll eat just as soon as your father gets here."

As Vonnie set out the brown stoneware plates and the silver she told her mother about Miss Hunt's request for an article for the school paper. "I'm really flattered that she asked me, especially since I'm not even in her journalism class."

"How nice, Vonnie. You're going to write it for her, aren't you?"

"I'll see how this first meeting goes. If it bombs, nobody's going to want to know more about graphology, and I'll be grossed out."

"Your meeting's not going to bomb. Anyway, I think graphology would make a good subject for an article under any circumstances. Most people are eager to learn more about themselves."

"How did your day go? I forgot to ask you. Did you finish a landscape?"

"Almost. I painted the skyline of the city from a vantage point near the freeway to Galveston. I still have more work to do on it, though. Maybe tomorrow."

When Mr. Morrison arrived, leather attaché in hand, Vonnie met him at the door. "Mom's fixed your favorite chicken casserole for dinner. How about that!"

"Yeah, how about it." He gave Vonnie a hug and began tugging at his tie. "I sense an excitement in the air. What could it be?"

"Oh, Dad! Don't put me on. You know the graphology club's meeting here tonight. We're ready for the countdown, and we're going to eat early."

"How could I have forgotten?"

Her father changed into slacks, sweater and loafers, and Vonnie was pleased that he hadn't donned the old gray sweats and Nikes that he usually wore around the house.

The conversation during dinner focused on graphology and the basic techniques Vonnie was going to stress that evening.

"We'll be right in the den if you need us," her dad said. "But I don't think you'll have any problems."

After they finished eating, Vonnie helped straighten the kitchen and load the dishwasher, then she put on her favorite jeans and blue sweater, old but comfortable.

Six-thirty. Six forty-five. At ten to seven her guests began to arrive, and Vonnie felt cool and ready to begin the meeting. Bob and Lora arrived first, bringing two girls from the junior class. Cass and Dick came in together, but Rod Jennings appeared alone, arriving just before two sophomore boys. Randy came alone also. Vonnie didn't ask where Monique was. Privately she thought they would have lucked out if Monique decided to boycott the group. Tish, too. Who needed them!

"Okay, gang." Vonnie stood at the card table waiting for the kids to stop chattering and wondering how to bring them to attention. She cleared her throat. "It's after seven. Let's begin the meeting with some intros. Starting with Dick, let's everyone say his name. I want you to know each other."

Dick stood, shouted his name like a carnival barker, then bowed. Although the rest of the kids laughed, they all remained seated and spoke more quietly. When the introductions were finished, Vonnie took charge again.

"I think the number-one thing we should do is to give the club a name. Any suggestions?"

"The graphology club," Dick offered in a deadpan voice. "That's what it is, isn't it? Let's not waste time trying to find a fancy handle."

"Perhaps you're right," Vonnie agreed, "but does anyone else have a suggestion?"

"We need a name with more snap," Cass said. "How about Write-On? The Write-On Club."

"Sounds like the title to a book I just read," Lora said, giggling.

"How about The Write Mode Club," Bob suggested. "That's a good name."

Rod groaned. "Hey, man, we're not going to be dealing with computer printouts. It's a pencil and paper thing."

"Then you think of something better," Bob said.

"The Lead with your Write Club," Randy said, breaking up the argument. "How's that?"

"Too long," Lora said. "What about The Write Gang?"

"The Write Gang." Vonnie repeated the words. "The Write Gang. It's clever. It's short. It describes us. What do the rest of you think?"

"Not bad." Bob gave his twin a thumbs-up sign. "Wish I'd thought of it first."

"Let's take a vote and get on with the meeting," one of the sophomores said.

"Maybe we should leave ourselves open to more ideas," Vonnie said. "I've written down the names you've mentioned so far. But let's not make too quick a decision."

"Good thinking," Rod said. "The name will stick with the club as long as it lasts. Sometimes rock groups decide on a name too quickly and then they regret it when they realize they're stuck with it. I know from experience. Why else do you think I'm playing with a group called The Greasy Cans?"

"Let's take our time deciding on a name," Lora said.

"Yeah," Cass agreed. "Let's leave it on the drawing board for now."

"Write down any other ideas you have and give them to me," Vonnie said. "We'll rap them at the next meeting and take a vote then."

"Let's get to the good stuff." Dick grinned at Vonnie, flexing his fingers like a concert pianist warming up for a performance. "Let's get to the writing. I want to hear you tell us about ourselves."

"The purpose of the club is not for *me* to tell you about yourselves," Vonnie said. "I want to teach *you* how to look at your writing or someone else's writing and see what it reveals."

"Whatever," Dick said. "But let's get on with it."

"Agreed." Vonnie opened a graphology book and peeked at her notes, then she looked at the group, ready to give them her full attention. "Everyone take paper and pencil and get in a comfortable writing position. If you want to pull your chairs up to this card table, fine. Maybe you'd rather use the dining-room table. The important thing is to take a comfortable and natural writing position."

Immediately the room looked like a jigsaw puzzle someone had accidentally kicked, sending the pieces flying, but everyone soon settled down with pencils poised over paper.

"What shall we write?" Cass twirled a strand of her red hair around her forefinger as if deep in thought.

Vonnie gave her usual reply. "Write about three lines of anything you choose, then sign your name. After that write numbers from one to ten."

"Spell them out?" Dick asked.

"No. Use numerals."

"Are you going to do this, too?" Lora asked. "Fair's fair. We want to see what your writing looks like."

"Okay." Vonnie took a piece of paper, sat at the card table and began writing.

"I can't think of anything to write," Dick said.

"And you were the one in such a hurry to get started." Bob thumped Dick lightly on the head with his ball-point. "Put your pen where your mouth is."

"Hey, guys. Cool it, okay?" Vonnie remembered all too well the time Dick had tricked Bob into falling fully clothed into Monique's swimming pool. There had been a rift between the two ever since, but she was determined to prevent any serious arguments tonight. "If you're really having trouble thinking of something to write, use the National Anthem or the Gettysburg Address. Anything will do."

"Four score and . . ." Dick began.

"Silently, you nerd," Bob said. "Don't be so V.D."

"Okay, gang," Vonnie said, irritated at Bob for picking up on one of Monique's latest expressions. "Time's up. Let's take a look at your writing."

"I'm looking. I'm looking," Cass said. "I wrote the words to 'The Eyes of Texas.'"

"Let's trade writing samples," Lora said.

Vonnie heard paper rip as Lora grabbed for Rod's paper, but he anchored it with both forearms, holding it securely in place in front of him.

"This time I'll ask everyone to look at his own writing," Vonnie said.

"Look for what?" Cass asked.

"First we'll notice some first-glance things. Size of writing, the pressure of pen or pencil. Those are starting points. Is the writing big or small? Is it dark and heavy? Is it light and faint? Or is it just rather ordinary looking?"

"What can we compare our sample to?" Randy asked.

Vonnie opened the graphology book to a page of examples. "Take a look. This explains it better than I can." She passed the book around, letting each person study the examples for a few moments before passing the book on.

"To really get into this subject, you may want to buy your own book," Vonnie said. "Of course, this isn't the only one on the market. There are quite a few graphology books available. If each of you bought a different book, we could share them."

"Got a list of titles?" Randy asked.

"Yes. I'll copy them and have them ready at the next meeting."

"We could even start our own small library," Lora said. "That would be fun."

"And keep it where?" someone called out.

"Maybe the school media specialist would give us shelf space if we asked her," Lora said. "That would keep the books handy for everyone to use."

"Let's talk about our writing," Dick said. "Everyone keeps getting off the subject. If we're going to learn things that can help us at home, at school and in the day-by-day business of living, let's get on with it. Why, my handwriting here may even explain my haircut."

Dick's tone was so pseudoserious that Vonnie was afraid his attitude might rub off on others and spoil the evening for everyone. She faked another smile and a laid-back approach.

"Your writing is one of a kind, Dick. Everyone's is. It's special. No two people have the same fingerprints or the same handwriting."

"My writing has heavy pressure," Rod said. "So what's that show?"

"Heavy pressure in writing may indicate a person with a great deal of energy. We've talked about that before. Athletes and business executives and people with creative minds often write with a heavy pressure."

"Well, I'm not athletic," Rod said. "So just call me creative. I like it. I like it."

"Maybe his writing is heavy because his hands are strong from playing keyboard," Lora said.

"My writing's very light," Cass said before anyone could comment on Lora's words. "I know I'm not athletic, but does it mean I'm not creative, either?"

"Light pressure may indicate that you're shy or reserved or that in present company you feel ill at ease."

"But I'm not any of those things," Cass insisted. "Really, I'm not and you all know it."

Vonnie had to agree with that. "Light pressure could also mean that you don't feel well or that you're in a mood to follow others rather than to lead the crowd. Handwriting can change with one's mood."

"I feel fine and my mood's fine, too."

"Don't worry, Cass," Lora said. "The world needs a few good followers. Leaders will end up in the unemployment lines if they can't find followers."

The group laughed, and Vonnie waited for them to quiet down again. "Now I want you to exchange papers for just a minute." She waited. "Look at the writing on the sheet you have. Is it easy to read or is it hard to read? Or is it somewhere in between easy and hard? Once you've decided, write that information at the bottom of the sheet and return the page to its owner."

"Hey!" Dick yelled at Cass. "You said my writing's hard to read."

"It is," Cass insisted. "Just look at it, Vonnie. It's all run together, both the words and the lines. Isn't it hard to read?"

"That was for you to decide, Cass. But I'll tell you what the experts say on the subject, then you and Dick can decide for yourselves what you think about it."

"Okay," Dick said. "But I can read it easily—so there!"

"Hard-to-read writing may indicate that you really dislike or fear being open with others. You may be too wrapped up in yourself, or you may just be a private sort of person who doesn't want others to know how he thinks or feels."

"I'm open with others," Dick said. "Totally open."

"Hah!" Randy said. "Practical jokers definitely aren't open with others. They're usually trying to be very sneaky and tricky."

"Well, I'm not wrapped up in myself," Dick said. "No way. I don't care what some dumb book says. It's wrong."

"No comment," Bob said.

"And I'm not a private sort of person," Dick said. "I think this graphology book is crazy. What happened to words like wonderful, super, magnificent. Let's hear something positive."

"You haven't heard the last part of the analysis," Vonnie said. "Hard-to-read writing may just mean that you write too fast. This's what I think happened to you, Dick. You were so eager to get on with the analysis that you rushed as you wrote. It's no big deal, but you can judge your writing better when you write more carefully."

"Know what I think?" Cass asked. "I think we should analyze writing we've done in the past when we weren't thinking about someone else trying to read things into it."

"A good point," Vonnie agreed.

"Right," Lora said. "I think graphology has a lot to offer and I definitely want to hear more, but how about writing anonymously?"

"We could put our samples in a box," Cass said, "then let you draw them out for us to study. Everybody's getting too uptight about all these personal comments."

"Everybody, meaning Dick Randall," Bob pointed out. "I haven't heard anyone else spouting off."

"Cass may have a good idea, at that." Vonnie shoved the graphology book aside. "It's sometimes hard to listen to personal criticism, and it's also tough to analyze writing when you know the person who wrote it. I think it would be a good idea to write anonymously next time. Each person would recognize his own writing and nobody else would be in the know."

"I've learned some things about myself here tonight," one of the new girls said. "Let's not let personal feelings slow the group down."

"Yeah," her friend agreed. "This is awesome stuff. I want to know more."

"Then let's look at the slant of the writing," Vonnie said, picking up on the positive comment. "The angle."

"Mine slants forward," Bob said.

"Mine slants to the left," one of the sophomores called out. "What's that mean?"

"There are seven types of angles," Vonnie said. "Take a look at this chart in the book and it'll help you understand." She held up the book. "We all know a right angle is ninety degrees. That's straight up and down. If the angle of your writing is to the left of the ninety-degree line, it could mean you are very reserved and probably timid."

"The farther back it slants, the more pronounced the trait, right?" Rod asked.

"Right," Vonnie agreed. "It could also mean the person is distrustful of others or that he has trouble facing the world or confronting his problems, whatever they are."

"My writing is straight up and down," Dick said. "What's the bad news about that?"

"It shows a person with a keen mind but who is rather insensitive to others." Vonnie smiled at Dick. "However these people are sincere and dependable. They make good friends."

"If you like insensitive friends," Bob said. "To each his own."

"The angle considered normal is the hundred-degree angle," Vonnie said. "People whose writing shows this angle are usually easygoing, friendly, calm and sensitive."

"Wow!" Lora said. "That's me. Look, Vonnie. Isn't that me?"

"It seems to be," Vonnie said. "But don't get carried away. It could also mean that you're just trying very hard to make your writing easy to read."

"You really know how to hurt a girl." Lora turned the paper over quickly, hiding it from Rod.

"I can't remember all this stuff," Randy said. "Maybe we're going too fast."

"Maybe we should bring notebooks and take notes," Cass said.

"No way," Dick said. "Sounds too much like school. We'll remember what we really need to remember, or what we're really interested in."

"Let's go on to other club matters right now," Vonnie said.

"Like what?" Lora rattled her paper, making a point of readying a fresh sheet. "I want to hear more about my writing."

Vonnie glanced at the clock, surprised to hear it strike the half hour. Eight-Thirty. An hour and a half was enough for one night. Leave them wanting more. She was ready to adjourn the meeting and bring out refreshments when they heard a knock.

Before Vonnie could reach the door, Monique pushed it open and stepped inside, bringing some cool night air with her. Her eyes blazed with excitement, holding Vonnie's attention until she noticed Tish had arrived, also.

"Glad you two made it," Dick called out. "Did you get mixed up on the time?"

"We've been to play practice," Monique said. "Tish and I tried out this afternoon and we both got big parts."

"Eat your heart out, Hollywood," Dick said. "Houston has first choice."

"Congratulations!" Vonnie looked at both girls. "That's neat."

"Thanks." Monique fluttered her eyelashes, showing off her frosted eye shadow. "We thought this meeting would be over by now. I've come to collect Randy so we can be on our way."

Vonnie saw Randy settle more firmly on the couch and sort of dig his heels into the carpet as if he had no intention of being collected. Drat. Why didn't they just go! She watched Tish settle beside Bob at the dining-room table.

"Won't you sit down, Monique?" Vonnie asked, amazed that her tongue could be saying stay while her mind was saying go. "We'll be having refreshments soon. Peppermint ice cream and chocolate chip cookies."

Monique remained standing. "Thanks, Vonnie, but Randy and I have previous plans for the rest of the evening." She took Randy's hand as if to pull him to his feet. "Come on, Randy. Let's go."

"Hold it a minute, Monique." He pulled his hand back and scooted over, making room for her to sit beside him. Monique scowled, but she sat down.

"Before we eat, I want to say one more thing," Vonnie said.

"Give," Lora said.

"Everyone's really been sort of uptight tonight. Let's try to mellow out next time. I want this to be a fun group."

Bob stood, walked away from Tish as he picked up the graphology book from the card table. "Vonnie's right. If we lighten up, everyone will have more fun. No problem. No big deal."

"Let's eat," Dick said. "That's the best part of any meeting."

"I'm for that," one of the sophomores called out. "Let's eat."

"I'll help you with the refreshments, Vonnie." Lora stood and turned toward the kitchen.

Monique stood, too, as if Vonnie had announced adjournment. "Let's go, Randy."

"You're welcome to say," Vonnie said.

"Refreshments!" Monique looked pained. "Good grief. You have to make goodies to bribe the kids to hang out with you?"

"Don't push it, Monique!" Randy glared at her.

"Yea, Monique," Cass said. "Put a cork in it. Nobody's bribing anyone to do anything."

Vonnie suddenly felt invisible. She opened her mouth to speak, but Monique had the floor.

"I think you're a bunch of phonies," Monique said. "It's a phony club based on a phony idea that handwriting reveals character." Monique picked up one of the dishes of mints Vonnie had placed in the room. "And the biggest phony of all is your leader. Look at this, kids." Monique held the candy out for all to see. "Candy."

"We've all seen candy before," Dick said.

"And so has Vonnie Morrison. She's trying to fool you all with her poor-little-sick-girl act. Diabetics can't have candy. Sweets are strictly off-limits for them. If Vonnie was really suffering from diabetes, she wouldn't have candy sitting around her house to tempt her." Monique set the candy back on the table. "Come on, gang." She snapped her fingers and winked. "Let's get out of here. Let's go somewhere and really have some fun."

Vonnie was speechless, barely controlling an urge to throttle Monique Wagar.

Five

Monique stood straighter, basking in the full attention of the group. She loved it! Even the sappy Vonnie Morrison was standing like a lump, lacking the grit to speak up for herself. It was like being on stage center in a play she had written and directed herself. She was holding her audience spellbound.

But the scene didn't last. Randy spoke first, and the others darted looks at one another and shifted in their chairs.

"Monique, you're out of line. Vonnie is a diabetic. She has her disease under control, but it's always a silent threat."

"Right," Lora said. "The mints are on hand for emergency use only. They keep the insulin under control. Right, Vonnie?"

"I don't believe in her phony emergencies," Monique said before Vonnie could reply. "I saw your Vonnie in action. Surely you remember my pool party. There was a test the next day and Vonnie felt duty bound to study. She faked a gross attack and went home while everyone else was still having loads of fun."

"Not true," Bob said. "She didn't have an attack. She recognized the onset of a problem in time to avoid it."

"You've all fallen for her poor-little-sick-girl act." Monique heard her voice shrill. "Now you're falling for her graphology! Bunko! V.D. It's a scam."

"I think you owe Vonnie an apology." Randy's quiet tone contrasted with the escalating volume of Monique's voice.

"Why?" Dick crumpled his paper and tossed it onto the card table where it bounced once, then hit the floor. "Monique has a right to her opinion. I don't know anything about diabetes, and after tonight I have a lot of doubts about graphology."

Monique glared at Dick for changing the subject. She had lost her audience. The spotlight had shifted to Dick.

"If I'm such an extrovert," Dick said, looking directly at Cass, "why am I always in the doghouse? People are supposed to like life-of-the-party types, aren't they?"

"People do like you," Cass said. "Who says they don't!"

"I don't," Bob said. "Jerks who push me into swimming pools with my clothes are on my hit list."

"I didn't push you," Dick said. "You fell."

"Same thing." Bob snorted. "You intentionally did it."

Monique knew she had lost her audience for good. Her best move now was to make a Pied Piper exit, taking lots of kids with her.

"Thanks for having the meeting, Vonnie," Randy said, letting Monique urge him toward the door. "We had fun."

"Right," Bob said. "Let's do it again soon."

"Sure," Vonnie said, looking directly at Bob and ignoring Monique. "Next time we'll study individual letter formations."

"Sounds fascinating," Monique said.

"You're all invited to stay for refreshments," Vonnie said again. "How about some cookies and ice cream?"

"No refreshments, thanks," Monique managed to nudge Tish into position beside Bob as they clustered at the door. "Need a ride, kids? I've got the car." She jingled her keys.

"No, thanks," Bob said. "I live close by."

"I drove Dad's car," Randy said.

"Leave it here for now," Monique said. "Come on. All three of you. Let's go to the pizzeria. It's time to celebrate."

"Celebrate?" Bob asked. "You came on like a big error message tonight. You break up our meeting. You insult Vonnie. And now you want to celebrate. I've had it. I'm going home."

"Oh, Bobby, don't be so straight." Monique linked her arm through Bob's, letting her hair brush his cheek, drawing him along with her. "Tish and I just weren't into graphology tonight."

"You made that quite obvious." Bob eased from Monique's side, standing closer to Tish.

"We're actresses." Monique kept heading toward the car. "Years from now we'll tell our fans how we got our start on the stage at Memorial High. We'll want to remember this night."

"Right," Tish agreed. "Let's live it up. This may be our last free time for ages. You should see our practice schedule!"

When they reached Monique's car, she hurried to open the door, knowing that the dome light shining on the red leather upholstery and the chrome trim would be hard for the guys to resist.

"Come on, gang. It's pizza time." She jingled the car keys in front of Randy. "How about driving? I need a break."

He took the keys, then slid beneath the wheel. "Ready?"

"Let's scoop a loop over to Westheimer," Monique snapped on the radio, tuning it up until the floor boards vibrated. "There's a neat pizza parlor near the drive-in movie. Very Italian."

Monique settled back, enjoying the ride, and she felt almost sorry when they reached Luigi's Pizzeria. But her mouth began to water as she smelled the oregano and tomato sauce.

Once inside the dimly lit building, they followed a waitress to a booth, placed their order and drank Cokes and listened to rock blaring from the jukebox while they waited.

"You're really not going back to another graphology meeting are you, Randy?" Monique asked when the music stopped.

"Why not? You're going with me, aren't you, Bob?"

"Right. Maybe if I learn enough about graphology I can psych out my family. They're coming from a different world."

"It's all a bunch of bunk," Monique said.

"You're really off base when you say that." A note of irritation sharpened Randy's voice. "You weren't even there for the whole meeting. Vonnie showed us some personality readings based on our handwriting that really seemed very accurate."

"True blue Vonnie," Monique said sarcastically.

The pizza arrived steaming an anchovy, cheese, and black olive scent all around them. Bob burned his tongue on the first bite and cooled his mouth with a gulp of water. While the others devoted their full attention to eating, Monique only nibbled at her piece, savoring the salty anchovy taste, remembering Glady's words about a diet, her own words about losing ten pounds. She wondered how Vonnie kept so thin.

"We haven't talked at all about the play," Monique said, ignoring the others and their chatter. "You're sitting here with future celebrities."

"Tell all," Bob said. "Will you have individual dressing rooms? Your names in lights?"

"Who knows!" Monique said. "It could happen."

"But probably not at Memorial High," Tish said.

They spent another half hour discussing the play, and it was after eleven when Bob pushed the empty pizza pan aside and insisted on going home. Reluctantly Monique slid from the booth. They had stayed long enough for lots of kids to see them. With any luck at all, the word would be around school tomorrow that Bob and Tish were an item. Eat your heart out, Vonnie Morrison, she thought.

Vonnie Morrison might know graphology, but she wasn't very good at hanging on to boyfriends. First she'd lost Randy. Now she was losing Bob. Monique could teach her a thing or two about boys. She wondered if Vonnie had ever deliberately flirted with a boy just to see what would happen.

After driving Tish and Bob home first, Monique then drove Randy to his car. When she arrived home, her parents were still out. So what else was new? She went to her room and was still working at her desk when Glady tapped on her door.

"Everything all right, Monique?"

"Sure, Glady. No sweat."

"It's past midnight." Glady held her watch to her ear as if she thought it might have stopped. "Don't study too late."

Monique almost broke up at that idea. "I won't, Glady." She laid papers she had collected where she would see them and remember to take them to school. Not likely that she'd forget! She couldn't remember when she'd had such a good idea.

The next day Monique's eyes felt like sand pits, and she could hardly hold them open through morning classes, but the thought of the lunchtime shock she was going to give Vonnie brought her alert at noon.

It surprised her to see Bob and Vonnie sitting together, as usual. What was the matter with Tish? The ball had been in Tish's court last night. She needed to give Tish some pointers.

"Hey, gang," she said as she placed her tray on the table and sat beside Randy. "I've got a great idea." She plunked her blue notebook in the center of the table and opened it with a flourish.

"What's up?" Randy asked.

"Look at this." Monique fanned three or four papers out on the table for them all to see.

"You're going to make a collage of your bad grades?" Cass asked. "Didn't know you were into Art Deco."

"Cassie, Cassie. Do let me explain." Monique paused, making the most of having used the nickname Cass hated and also making sure she had everyone's full attention. Even Vonnie's. Especially Vonnie's. "You may see nothing more here than negative comments on these sheets, but I see something far more important."

"What?" Lora asked.

"Handwriting," Monique said. "Unique and individual."

"Meaning what?" Randy asked.

"Teachers' handwriting."

Dick reached for one of the papers that had lots of red-ink writing in the top and bottom margins. "Teachers' handwriting! Neato, Monique. You're thinking we can zero in on this writing and learn what makes those suckers tick."

"Something like that," Monique admitted, "if you're into crudeness. But if we're going to have a graphology group, then let's give it a little pizzazz, a little glitz."

"Thought you weren't interested in graphology," Lora said.

"Hey, let's see that English theme." Bob reached for the paper. "What can this marginal writing tell us about Baller?"

"The writing slants uphill," Cass said. "That means she's optimistic. And it's boldly written."

"Shows strength and energy," Lora said. "Isn't that right?"

"She's too little to have much strength," Monique said. "What do you think, Vonnie?" She turned to see how Vonnie was adapting to taking a back seat.

Vonnie hesitated.

"What's the matter?" Randy asked. "You see something bad?"

"Not especially," Vonnie said. "I just don't like talking about someone's writing when that someone's absent. Seems unfair."

"Don't be such a goody two-shoes!" Monique said. "Who cares about fair?"

"Come on, Von," Randy said. "This is fun. You know what I'm going to do when I learn more about graphology? I'm going to sneak writing from our football opponents. I'll analyze their script and freak them out."

"Graphology could open up a whole new area of scouting," Bob said. "Remember you heard it here first."

Monique pushed Miss Baller's writing toward Vonnie, determined to put her on the spot. "What do you see, Vonnie?"

Vonnie shoved the paper away.

"You're afraid," Monique taunted. "You're chicken."

"Come on, Vonnie," Bob urged. "Give. Maybe we can get the inside track with old Baller and raise our English grades."

"Right," Monique said. "I may have the key to straight A's."

"I just want to know a few of Baller's deep-hidden secrets," Randy said. "What do you see, Von?"

"Okay." Vonnie laid the sheet in front of her. "First, let's notice how she crosses her *t*'s."

"They looked crossed well enough to me," Dick said.

"Right," Vonnie agreed. "They're all carefully crossed. The cross bar equally divides the stem of the letter and it sits midway between top and bottom of that stem."

"So what's it mean?" Rod asked, taking Lora's hand and holding it under the table.

"Use logic in your observations," Vonnie said. "Care in writing details denotes care in everyday activities. The *t* bars show that Miss Baller is careful about details."

"Maybe that's just how her teacher taught her to make *t* bars when she was learning to write," Lora said.

"That could be," Vonnie admitted. "But in spite of early penmanship lessons, character shines through a person's writing."

Dick pulled his history paper from his shirt pocket. "Look at my *t* bars." He pointed to them. "They're off to the right of the letter stem. Most of them don't even touch the stem."

"So what does that tell us?" Vonnie asked.

"That he's careless about details," Cass said.

"Be real," Bob said. "He's a slob. I knew it all the time. And now he presents us with the proof."

"No fair." Dick grabbed his paper back. "Let's see your *t* bars, buddy. I'm guessing you aren't all that neat, either."

"I don't have any writing with me," Bob said. "The computer makes most of my *t* bars these days."

Dick turned his history paper over and shoved it toward Bob. "Write some words with the letter *t* in them. Lots of them."

Slowly Bob wrote a few lines, biting his lower lip as he concentrated.

"You're faking it," Monique said. "No fair. Now that you know what careless *t* bars mean, you're trying for perfection."

"Who says?" Rod asked. "It just shows us that Bob cares what we think of him."

"For a short time a person may be able to make his writing show things that aren't really true," Vonnie said. "But natural rhythms and nuances will show up in the long run. Changing your handwriting is about as easy as changing your fingerprints."

"So forget faking it," Monique said. "Look at this. I've got a sample of Buckner's writing. The Whip. Want to see?"

"Where'd you get it?" Rod asked.

"From a note to my parents," Monique said.

"Pessimistic," Dick said. "Slants downhill."

"Vice principals have reason to be pessimistic," Bob said. "All they ever see are the hard cases."

"Not so," Dick said. "He sees me a lot."

"I rest my case," Bob said.

"Look at that writing," Tish said. "All the *o*'s and *a*'s are open at the top. What's that mean, Vonnie?"

"It could mean that the person's rather talkative," Vonnie said, "that he's open and eager to communicate. It also could mean that he's open-minded and willing to listen to others."

"That figures," Monique said. "That's why Buckner's on the intercom interrupting classes all the time with announcements."

Before Vonnie could say more, the bell rang and everyone stood. Monique felt pleased. She had held everyone's attention more easily than Vonnie had. Vonnie might know graphology, but Monique Wagar, successful actress, knew people.

"Guys, I've changed my mind about graphology," Monique told the group. "I think there may be something to it, after all."

"That's a real switch from last night," Lora said.

"I like getting the scoop on the teachers." Monique winked. "I could use some A's, and there're a few guys I'd like to psyche out, too."

Monique was about to join Randy in leaving the lunchroom when Vonnie spoke.

"I need to talk to you, Monique. Privately. After school."

"I've got play practice."

"Immediately after?"

"Well, it takes Baller a while to get organized. She's meticulous about details, remember? You discovered that fact right on my red-F English theme."

"I'll meet you near the English room right after school," Vonnie said.

"Okay." Monique sensed trouble, but she refused to let Vonnie bluff her. "You'll have to make it brief. I'm on at the beginning of each act. They can't start practice without me."

Monique spent the afternoon wondering what Vonnie wanted to discuss with her. When she headed for the English room she thought she knew, but she wasn't sure. Was it her imagination, or had Vonnie actually grown a bit pale when she saw Miss Baller's handwriting? She would have to move carefully. She didn't want to get on Vonnie's hit list—at least not too soon.

Vonnie had info she needed. The things Vonnie had said about Miss Baller and Mr. Buckner were true. If handwriting could really reveal personal information, Monique could use some of Vonnie's know-how. Was her dad really a Scrooge? Maybe if she studied his writing she could find a weakness she could tap to get a reprieve on the no-new-clothes rule. It was worth a try. And was her mother really a shoo-in for socialite of the year? Maybe something in her writing would show Monique how to reach her.

Monique was still thinking about those possibilities when she saw Vonnie approaching the English room.

"The auditorium's still empty." Monique led the way to the auditorium and took a seat. Vonnie remained standing.

"What I have to say won't take long. I don't like the way things were going at lunch, Monique. I don't think we should be analyzing the teachers' handwriting."

"Why not? It's not copyrighted. It's right there on my paper for me and anyone else to see."

"I think we could get in big trouble."

Monique laughed. Vonnie was as transparent as Saran Wrap. "You're faking me out, Vonnie. That's not what you're really afraid of and you know it." Monique knew for sure she had hit home when she saw Vonnie's face flush. "You'd like to analyze the teachers' writing just as much as the rest of us would."

"Okay," Vonnie admitted. "Maybe so. But you're faking the group out when you talk about the analysis helping to improve grades," Vonnie said. "You don't care anything about grades."

Monique stood. It was hard to make her point with Vonnie towering over her. "So you're faking it about trouble and I'm faking it about grades. Let's level with each other,

Vonnie. You're not worried about our dear teachers and their feelings. You're holding back because you see me taking over the group, don't you? The kids are paying more attention to my ideas than they are to yours."

"That's not true!"

"Then why are you so wired now?" Monique chuckled. "You have trouble hanging on to things, don't you? Randy. Bob. Bob was with Tish after the meeting last night. Ask him about the pizza over on Westheimer. And now you can't even hang on to your own graphology group."

"That's not true."

"Of course it's true. I had the gang's full attention this noon, and you could hardly stand it."

"But you don't know anything about graphology. All you know is what I've told you, what I've helped you learn."

"That's true, but I can be a quick study when I want to."

"You messed up with the Super Seniors club, so why don't you just ease off and let me manage the group my own way?"

"I'm just getting even with you for dating Randy while I was in France. I don't like being upstaged."

"I didn't know anything about you when I first went out with Randy. And when I found out, I dropped him before he could drop me. But all that has nothing to do with graphology. I think we're going to get into big trouble with your tacky ideas."

"If you're so afraid of working behind the teachers' backs, let's open the club to teachers. Let's invite them to attend the meetings. Let's make them welcome."

"You've got to be kidding!" Vonnie took a step toward Monique. "Who needs more teachers! We get enough of them in classes without inviting them to our after-hours meetings."

"Thank goodness you're sharp enough to see that. I don't really want teachers invited into the club. I just wanted to see your reaction to the idea. You're not as straight as I imagined. I thought you'd go for the teacher invite idea."

"No way."

"Well, hear this. I'm attending the next meeting. I'm bringing more faculty handwriting samples. I'm taking over the group and you can't stop me."

Vonnie turned and left the auditorium, but Monique knew she had made her point. Vonnie might have the graphology know-how, but she, Monique had the sharp ideas that attracted the gang and kept them looking up to her for a good time. Who needed Vonnie?

Six

Vonnie had thought a good night's sleep would brighten her outlook concerning Monique and the graphology group. But it hadn't. Her eyes felt grainy, and she wished she could skip school just this once. Who needed all this grief! Monique had X-ray vision. Vonnie could see through all her ploys to keep the upper hand in the graphology club. Why had she ever become involved in that club, anyway? She wished she could forget all about the whole thing, but she could hardly pick up her marbles and go home now without looking like a sorehead and a quitter. She had been V.D.—very dumb to get involved in the first place.

At noon Bob called to her, then began following her down the hall as she started to leave the school building. "Wait up. Where you going?"

"Home for lunch." Vonnie walked on toward the door, wishing she couldn't smell the enticing fragrance of chili. "Most of today's menu's off-limits for my diet." To her surprise Bob said nothing more and he dashed off toward the cafeteria. Maybe Bob could see right through her, too. Maybe it didn't even take X-ray vision.

She heard Bob shout to Lora and listened to the sounds of Dick's laughter coming from the lunchroom. Bob probably doesn't want to miss a minute of Monique's fascinating comments, she thought. But before she reached the end of the first block she heard shoe soles slapping concrete, and in a few seconds Bob joined her carrying a cheese sandwich, an apple and a bottle of soda.

"Want some company for lunch?"

"Sure. I absolutely hate eating alone, and I know Mom'll be out painting. We can pull the patio table and chairs into the sun and really enjoy our break."

Bob tossed the apple in the air, caught it in one hand, tossed it again. "This is a cop-out, you know."

"Meaning what?"

"You know what I mean. You've never had many problems finding something on the school menu that's also on your diet. Apple. Milk. Cheese. Crackers. Soup. And today they're serving chili. You can eat that without any big problem, can't you?"

"Where is it written that I have to eat at school? I just thought I'd go home for a change."

"For a change from Monique?"

Vonnie walked faster. Why hadn't Bob just stayed with the gang? Nothing wrong with a girl going home for lunch now and then. No big deal.

"Vonnie, I really don't see why you and Monique can't get along."

"That's easy for you to say."

"What's the big problem between you two? Are you jealous because she's got a leading part in the play?"

"Of course not. Why would I be jealous of that?"

"I don't know. That's for sure. Just thought you might be. You ever been in a play?"

"No. I worked with the lighting crew on one when we lived in Roe Village. I just ran a spotlight. No big deal. I just had to keep the light focused on the person who was currently speaking lines."

"Sounds like it might be fun."

"Right. And it was a lot easier than learning lines."

"Can't you try a little harder to get along with Monique? I mean, with you two at odds, it makes for some uneasy feelings in the gang."

"How can I get along with her when she's out for revenge?"

"Revenge for what? I can't see that you've done anything to her that demands revenge."

"Right. I haven't. But Monique doesn't see it that way, Bob. She told me so. She said . . ."

"Spare me the gruesome details. I'm sorry I asked." Bob bit into the apple and chewed thoughtfully. "No matter what she did, no matter what you did, why don't you just try to get along?"

"The way you and Dick do? Try thinking about how you feel toward Dick and you might be able to understand how I feel toward Monique."

"Dick and I keep our cool," Bob said. "We jab each other now and then, and I look out for my own interests in any matter that concerns us both, but basically we understand each other. You know why?"

"I'm dying to know." Vonnie turned onto the narrow walk leading to her front door and hurried onto the porch.

"Dick and I can share space because I make a lot of allowances for his immaturity. He's a child. When I remember that, I can give him more room."

"Big of you, Bob. Really big. But all that has nothing at all to do with Monique and me. She's not a child, and I've given her too much space already. Can't you see what she's trying to do?"

"Monique's just out for some laughs. Fun's her big thing. She has a talent for it. It's like Dick's pastime of playing rotten jokes on unsuspecting victims and it's like my thing of learning about computers."

"Monique's out to take over the graphology club, that's what she's trying to do."

"So why do you feel so threatened, Vonnie? Monique can't take over. She doesn't have the know-how. The gang asked you to lead the club and they haven't changed their minds about that. They really look up to you."

"But they won't for long. Not if Monique has her way about it."

"Of course they will. You have the solid info that's necessary to keep the club going. Monique's interest is shallow. She just manages to have the . . . the . . ."

"The fun ideas." Vonnie finished the sentence for him as they stepped inside the house.

"Right. Monique does have fun ideas, but a club can't operate totally on fun ideas."

"Her followers seem willing to try. They were a lot more interested in analyzing the teachers' writing than they were in analyzing their own. You saw how uptight everyone got at the meeting. Especially Dick. I just knew Dick was going to pitch me a fit."

"Everyone felt self-conscious doing something so new and different. At least I did. It's really hard to reveal private things about yourself, and at a public meeting, it can happen so fast that you've got no time to prepare a defense."

"Nobody was on trial. Except maybe me as a leader." Vonnie headed toward the refrigerator.

"It's hard to be open about personal matters. It's a lot easier to look at some teacher's writing and talk about that. I think the gang latched on to Monique's idea as a way to direct attention away from themselves."

"I suppose so."

"But you can bet all the kids were thinking the same things Dick was thinking."

"What do you mean?"

"They were looking at Miss Baller's *t* bars, but they were applying the things you said to their own writing. Dick just happened to be the only one outgoing enough to mention it. That guy doesn't care what he says."

Vonnie pulled milk, cottage cheese and fruit from the refrigerator, then led the way through the back door to the patio.

"Want some cottage cheese?" she offered as she opened the umbrella above the patio table.

"No, thanks. This sandwich is plenty."

Vonnie watched palm fronds sway in a gentle breeze, listened to their quiet whisper as she and Bob ate without speaking for a few moments.

"You may be right, Bob," Vonnie said at last. "Maybe we do need Monique and her ideas to keep the whole club scene from getting too heavy. Monique and Dick."

"The comic relief. If you can look at it that way, I think the club meetings will move along smoothly and be fun for everyone."

"Thanks, Bob."

"Thanks for nothing."

"No, I mean it. You've helped me over a big hump. If you can take Dick in stride after all the mean tricks he's played on you, I can surely learn to tolerate Monique."

"We'll rise above them like balloons rising above the clouds."

"Right. And my grandmother used to say that cream always rises to the top."

"So uncool," Bob said. "So very uncool. I'd rather be a balloon than a glob of cream any day of the week."

"Yeah, me too." She glanced at her watch. "We'd better be getting back. Suppose the gang wondered where we were?"

"Of course they wondered. No doubt about that. But they've probably been analyzing some other teacher's *t* bars and open *a*'s and we've missed out on the fun."

"Big deal." Vonnie put her dishes in the dishwasher, and they headed back to school. "Bob, I've got an idea I'd like to run by you."

"Give."

"Miss Hunt has asked me to write an article about graphology for *The Iconoclast*."

"Good deal. And you're not even in her journalism class! She seldom asks for outside help."

"Well, I've got this neat plan. At least I think it's neat, and I want your opinion."

"Flattery will get you everywhere."

"No flattery involved. Here's the idea. I'll just write a brief explanation of graphology and its uses, then I'll show some actual examples of student writing and analyze them in a general sort of way. And I'll keep it pleasant. Nothing negative."

"Sounds good. Whose writing will you use?"

"That's the big deal. I want to get writing samples from some members of the play cast. I mean I'd like to get them today."

"Why the big hurry?"

"I want samples that show their writing before they get deeply involved in the characters they're playing on stage. Then I want to wait a week or so and get fresh samples."

"After they've gotten more involved in their characters, right?"

"You've got it. If my theories are correct, the writing samples should show some changes."

"Really?"

"I think so. Minor differences, maybe, but nobody's character or personality is set in marble. We all change. Our moods go up and down from day to day, even from hour to hour. I think the before and after handwriting samples from the cast will show some changes that could make some interesting points about graphology."

"Great idea, Vonnie! An article like that should really grab the whole student body. It'll have every person in school taking a closer look at his handwriting—students and teachers."

"Glad you like the idea, Bob. You give me confidence. It'll be easier to ask for Miss Hunt's opinion now that I have the opinion of one reader."

They reached the school just as the bell rang for afternoon classes. History. Chemistry. The building seemed stuffy after being outside, and Vonnie opened a window in the history room. As class got under way she managed to keep her mind on Civil War battles, but just barely.

When school was dismissed for the day, she hurried to Miss Hunt's journalism room. This time she bypassed the seats in the back row and stood near the teacher's desk, obviously waiting for her attention.

"Vonnie," Miss Hunt said. "Sit down a moment, please."

"Sorry, Miss Hunt. I have to get right home. Do you have a second to talk with me? In private?"

Miss Hunt raised an eyebrow in surprise, but she nodded. "Come on into my office."

Vonnie followed her into a tiny cubicle of a room that smelled of printers' ink and new paper, but at least they were alone. Miss Hunt sat at her desk, but Vonnie remained standing as she presented her idea much as she had laid it out earlier for Bob.

"What do you think?" Vonnie asked when she finished.

"Sounds like a lot of work, getting all those writing samples along with releases to use them. Each person's permission would be required."

"I think the finished article would be worth the work. The kids would like the idea, and the article would give them some leads on analyzing their own writing."

"Agreed. And if you're willing to do the footwork, I'll go along with the plan. But remember the deadline." Miss Hunt stood. "I'm a stickler for deadlines."

"I will." Vonnie turned toward the door. "I'll have it to you in plenty of time for the next issue."

Vonnie left the journalism department feeling confident that she could produce the article she had promised. This was going to be fun. She looked forward to the new challenge as she imagined her article in print, the title over her byline. Byline. Exciting! Title? Did writers write the title before or after they wrote their articles?

She and Lora walked home from school together, as usual, but she didn't tell Lora about the article. It would lose its element of surprise if she shared the idea with too many kids. And if she talked about it too much, it would lessen her enthusiasm for writing it.

As soon as she got home, she went straight to her room to begin the first part of the article. Should she write it on the typewriter? She fed a page of paper into the machine, set the margins, the tab. And she stared at the blank sheet. Where were the words she needed?

The typewriter bugged her. She didn't really feel at home with it. Pulling out pen and paper, she began to rough draft the article in longhand. Six hundred words. She wrote. She scratched out. She wrote again. Two hours had passed before she laid the sheets aside, knowing that the material needed to cool a day or so before she tackled another revision. But she was on her way. Now all she had to think about was getting the necessary writing samples.

How was she going to do that? Monique? Tish? They were her only contacts with the play cast, but the thought of asking either of them for help made her cringe. The article might turn out just like the graphology club. Monique might try to take over. She wasn't about to let that happen. She would show Bob she could deal with Monique just as well as he could deal with Dick, and this was a good time to begin.

The next day Vonnie stayed for school lunch. The gang was seated in its regular place when they saw Tish approaching with a new boy in tow. Medium height. Muscular. Red hair short in front, long in back and blending into a rattail that hung over his T-shirt.

"Who's the dreamboat?" Cass asked. "Anyone seen him around here before?"

"He doesn't look so dreamy to me," Dick said. "Not my type at all."

"I'd be disappointed if you weren't a little jealous," Cass said. "I was just testing."

"If he gives you the eye, I'll deck him." Dick banged his fist on the table for emphasis.

"Knock it off, man," Rod said. "He's with Tish, remember?"

"She didn't tell me anything about a new guy," Monique said.

"And of course she tells you all," Lora said.

"Well, we were together at play practice last night. I drove her home afterward."

"Maybe she was afraid you'd latch on to him," Cass said. "Stranger things have happened."

"Cassie, Cassie," Monique said. "I've never been known to latch on to a guy. Latching on to has never been a necessity in my life. I'm much more subtle than that."

"He's a hunk," Lora said.

"I think new cowboy boots are uncool," Rod said. "Too Texas to really be Texas."

"He's not very tall in the saddle," Lora said. "But he looks nice."

"Big deal," Rod said. "Who needs him?"

"Tish, maybe," Vonnie said. "I think they make a nice-looking couple." She hoped nobody would guess how it relieved her to see Tish interested in some boy other than Bob.

"Shh," Lora said. "Here they come." She scooted over to make more room, and Randy helped pull extra chairs to the table. They all eased their trays together to make room for two more.

"Thanks, Randy," Tish said. "Gang, I'd like you to meet Chet Rolf. He's a senior and he's just moved here from Lake City." Tish introduced them all by name, and Chet smiled a greeting, acting as if introductions made him wary. Vonnie wondered if he was wary or just shy.

"How come you've moved here?" Dick asked.

Chet eyed Dick's Mohawk, then met his gaze. "My family moved here. Why else?"

"Good reason," Vonnie said. "It happens to us all sooner or later."

"Yeah," Bob agreed. "I don't think any of us have lived in Houston all our lives."

"You play ball?" Randy asked.

"No." Chet gave his full attention to his meat loaf and salad.

"You into music?" Rod asked.

"I listen to an album now and then," Chet replied. "Springsteen. Beatles' oldies. Rod Stewart."

"Got your class schedule?" Monique asked, looking at some papers that Chet had stuffed into his shirt pocket.

"Yeah. Tish's supposed to show me around the building. I've written down some directions and room numbers."

Monique leaned forward. "Let me take a look, okay? Sometimes I know some shortcuts that can save a lot of time between classes."

Vonnie squelched a sigh as Chet pulled the papers from his pocket and slapped them onto the table in front of Monique. "Can a guy get seconds around here? I'm still starving."

"You'll have to use another lunch ticket," Tish said. "Either that or go through the sandwich line. Come on. I'll go with you."

Once they'd left the table, Monique pounced on Chet's papers. "He's not going to be a mystery man for long, kids. Let's see what we can learn about him."

"Help us, Vonnie," Lora said, pulling the paper into a position that let them see it better.

"The writing lines are level," Dick said. "They don't slant up. They don't slant down. What's that mean, Vonnie? We haven't talked about that yet."

"Maybe it just means he's upset about starting in a new school," Cass said. "What do you see, Vonnie?" She slid the paper from under Lora's fingers and pushed it in front of Vonnie.

"Level lines usually show a determination to succeed," Vonnie said. "He could be a person who moves in fast forward toward his goals."

"Wonder what he wants to succeed at," Rod said.

"Look at the size of his writing." Vonnie pointed to the top lines on the page. "It's large. That usually shows a person who is very active and sometimes very revved up and restless."

"He sounds like a character from the soaps," Lora said. "Wonder why his writing slants to the left."

"Good point," Vonnie said. "Most people's writing slants to the right at least a little bit. When I see a left slant I think of a shy person who is distrustful of others or who is afraid of facing the world."

"Maybe he's just bummed about facing a new school," Bob said. "Give the guy a break. Maybe he's a little timid."

"Right," Cass said. "Good thinking. But look at how widely spaced his letters are. Does that mean anything?"

"Wide spacing can fool you," Vonnie said. "Many graphologists believe that wide spacing shows a fine mind at work."

"You mean this guy's a genius, maybe?" Dick asked. "And I was about to like him!"

"Wide spacing can mean a variety of things," Vonnie said. "The graphology books I have show writing samples of great people, and lots of them wrote widely spaced letters."

Vonnie tapped the paper. "Wide spacing sometimes shows a feeling of importance. In this writing, the spaces are even and that shows a person with good judgment and a big imagination."

"Enough." Monique slid the paper back where it had been before Chet left the table. "They're coming back."

When Chet and Tish joined the group again, nobody spoke for a moment, and Vonnie felt overly conscious of the silence. Surely Chet would guess they had been talking about him.

"How's play practice going, Monique?" she asked.

"Just great. Miss Baller says this cast is really with it." Monique nudged Tish. "Isn't that what she said, Tish?"

"Right," Tish agreed. "She thinks we have a natural feel for the stage."

"What's that supposed to mean?" Dick asked. "Sounds like a bunch of flattery to me. She's probably just trying to make you work harder. Teachers are sneaky that way. You have to watch out for it every minute."

"I shouldn't think you'd have to worry too much," Bob said.

"Monique, I need to talk to you," Vonnie said.

"So talk." Monique met Vonnie's gaze as if daring her to say another word.

"In private," Vonnie said.

"Again?" Monique asked. "It's getting to be a habit."

"Pardon the rest of us for living," Dick said. "The girls want privacy."

Monique rose, clearly curious about Vonnie's plans. "Come with me, Vonnie. I need to get some stuff from my locker. We can talk on the way."

Dishes clattered as they carried their trays to the conveyor belt, and as they left the cafeteria, Vonnie hoped Bob was noticing her new attitude toward Monique. She tried to plan her words, her request, carefully so Monique would be flattered.

"I could use your help with a project I'm working on, Monique."

"You still worried about your graphology club?"

"No. I'm not worried about it at all." Vonnie felt heat on her neck that threatened to rise to her face. She wasn't good at lying. "I need your help on another matter that's come up just recently."

"So tell me about it." Monique led the way to a window ledge at the end of the senior hall, hoisted herself onto it and waited for Vonnie to join her.

Vonnie sat beside Monique, feeling the coolness of the concrete seep through her denim skirt. "I'm writing an article for the school paper."

"And you expect my help? You've seen some of my English grades. Be real, Vonnie."

"This has nothing to do with grades. But it does have to do with the play and the play cast." She smelled Monique's cloyingly sweet perfume as Monique leaned toward her.

"Give. You want to help backstage? You're writing a personal experience article?"

"No. I want you to help me get writing samples from some of the cast."

"What's the deal?"

Vonnie explained her article idea to Monique, hoping she hadn't made a mistake in revealing it. For a few moments Monique said nothing, then she smiled.

"That's a neat idea. Very neat."

"Then you'll help me get the samples? It's not going to be all that easy."

"Of course it'll be easy. I know the cast members. I'll just introduce you and we'll ask them to write for us." Monique leaned toward Vonnie. "Will you use some of my writing? Will I get to see it in the paper?"

"Hold it, Monique. Yes, I'll use some of your writing if you'll let me, but we're going to have to get true samples."

"True samples. What's that supposed to mean?"

"At the club meeting I just asked the kids to write something on the spur of the moment. But that's not the best kind of writing to try to analyze. Sometimes people tense up when they know their writing is going to be under scrutiny.''

''That figures,'' Monique said.

''So for this article, I'd like to get samples that have been written in the near past when the person was at ease. Old writing. You know what I mean.''

''Right.''

''Then, after a few days of play practice, I'd like to get another writing sample that was done when the person was in a relaxed mood. Maybe a piece of homework or something like that, but nothing that was done especially for analysis. Think you can help?''

''Sure,'' Monique said. ''How many kids do you want samples from?''

''I'm not sure yet. Maybe three girls and three boys. But I may not use them all in the article. I just want enough to have a fair sample to choose from.''

''Tell you what. Why don't you meet me after play practice today and we'll talk to some of the kids.''

''Okay. Sounds good.'' Vonnie slid from her perch on the window ledge then looked up at Monique. ''Thanks a bunch, Monique. I didn't know whether you'd help or not. You'll make the job a lot easier for me.''

''Just be sure my writing sample makes it into the article. It's not easy to get your name in the paper in this school unless you're an athlete or a musician or a brain or something. They haven't even given the play cast any ink yet. Do you think that's fair?''

''The cast will get some publicity. Be patient.'' Vonnie knew Monique's words were true. The people whose names were in the paper were usually people who were taking part in activities, making the honor roll, or coming up with new ideas for student government. That usually excluded Monique. No wonder Monique was being so cooperative. They needed each other.

Seven

Monique watched as Vonnie settled in a back seat to view the afternoon rehearsal, then she hurried backstage to find Tish. The faint smell of greasepaint clinging to the heavy curtains gave her the feeling of really being into theater.

"Tish, guess what." Monique began coiling her long hair and pulling it onto the top of her head in a golden crown.

"Baller isn't requiring any costuming at this point," Tish said. "Why the hairdo?"

"I'm trying to get into my character. I feel more sophisticated with my hair up. Guess what, Tish?"

"Vonnie's out front." Tish yawned.

"And guess what else?" Monique checked her image in a wall mirror.

"I'm not into guessing games."

"So I'll tell you. Vonnie came to me for help. She was almost groveling. It was great."

"What sort of help?" Tish gave Monique her full attention.

"Hear this." Monique told Tish briefly about Vonnie's plans for the graphology article. "We're both going to have our names and our handwriting in *The Iconoclast*."

"That's cool." Tish fanned herself with her play book, fluffing her short bangs as she stirred the stuffy backstage air.

"You'll give her a sample of your writing, won't you?"

"Sure. It never hurts to have your name in the paper."

"All actors on stage for the first act," Miss Baller called.

Monique wondered if famous actresses could taste fame. Every time she stepped onstage she got a rusty taste in the back of her mouth. Maybe it was just nerves.

Miss Baller had them read through the first and second acts, finding their places on the set as they went along. Monique forgot about Vonnie until the practice ended and she approached.

"Have you talked to anyone yet?" Vonnie admired Monique's upswept hairstyle and stage makeup.

"I've only mentioned the article to Tish so far. She's interested. Let's go talk to some of the guys right now."

Monique headed toward Jason Grover and Ryan Smith. She didn't know them as well, but what better time to get acquainted? Where had Miss Baller found them? Average height. Slim. Brown hair. Brown eyes. Ryan wore thick-lensed glasses. Jason wore braces. Could the makeup crew give these two glamor?

"Hey, guys, have I ever got a deal for you." Monique looked up at both boys through her thick fringe of lashes, smiled, then basked in their full attention. A glance from the corner of her eye told her that Vonnie was impressed.

"What's the word?" Jason folded his play book and rammed it into the hip pocket of his jeans, keeping his gaze on Monique.

Ryan rocked on his heels, saying nothing.

"I need your autographs," Monique made her voice whispery.

"You're kidding," Jason said.

"Yeah, I am." She put her hand on his arm. "I need more than an autograph. Come with me."

Monique introduced the boys to Vonnie and explained about the graphology article. "If you'll cooperate, you'll get your names and your handwriting in the school paper. Just give us an old page of homework, okay?" Again she looked up at the boys.

"Sounds weird," Jason said.

"But it'll be good publicity for the play—and for us," Monique pointed out. She pulled a white sack of cinnamon drops from her shoulder bag. Bribery. It worked. They accepted the candy and popped it into their mouths. The spicy scent soon hung in the air as they began searching for some writing samples.

Paper rustled. Notebook rings clicked. Ryan was first to produce part of an English theme, then Jason gave Monique some dog-eared notes he had taken at the library.

"Do we get to see what you write about us before it's published?" Ryan asked. "This could be invasion of privacy."

I'll give you a preview," Vonnie promised, heading for the door before either boy could change his mind.

"Who would you rather have invade your privacy than us?" Monique winked at them then she pulled Vonnie toward a short dark-haired boy who was about to leave the stage.

"Hey, Mike," she called. "Listen up a minute, okay? You too, Deedee."

Mike and Deedee paused, listened to Monique's request, then they supplied writing samples.

"And there you have them," Monique said as she and Vonnie left the stage. "I'll get Tish's for you tomorrow."

"Thanks, Monique. Thanks a bunch. I'll see you later."

"Hold on one little minute. Aren't you...aren't we going to take a look at the writing samples?" Monique crunched the remainder of her cinnamon ball, swallowing quickly to relieve her burning tongue.

"Why, sure. We can look at them now if you're interested."

"Sure I'm interested. Jason and Ryan seem like okay guys. Mike, too. I like his looks, don't you?" She hated being forced to pursue Vonnie, but she had little choice. "Let's go to my house and examine the samples."

Vonnie looked at her watch. "Can't do it, Monique. We eat right at six o'clock."

"So you've got an hour."

"No, not really. I have to get home and help Mom with the meal. We share the work and she'll be expecting me."

"So eat a little late tonight. We never eat before seven at our house. Sometimes it's seven-thirty or eight." Drat Vonnie, making her beg this way! Vonnie could afford to call the shots now that she had what she wanted.

"I have to keep on schedule," Vonnie said. "Sorry. We can look the writing samples over sometime tomorrow."

"Tonight," Monique insisted. "I'll pick you up after dinner and we can go to my house."

"If we're going to get together, why don't we just stay at my house, Monique?"

Monique began to see another side to Vonnie. She hid some backbone under her poor-little-sick-girl act. "Okay, Vonnie. I'll be there around eight. Is that all right?"

"Fine. See you then." Vonnie turned to leave.

"Want a ride home?" Even a small thing like a lift home would put Vonnie a bit more in her debt. That's the way she liked to keep people, a little bit beholden to her.

"Thanks for the offer," Vonnie said, leaving the building, "but I need the exercise of walking."

She's jealous, Monique thought—jealous of my car, my house, my play cast connections. Monique slid under the wheel of her Camaro and started the motor. Or maybe she was just wary. Maybe she couldn't forget the Super Seniors, the shoplifting fiasco. Cautious little Vonnie.

Once she got home Monique found a note from Glady.

Dear Monique, Herman and I have gone to a game at the Astrodome. Your dinner's in the refrig. We'll be home early. Your parents are at a concert at Jones Hall. They'll be in very late. Best, Glady.

Monique crumpled the note. "Nice that everyone's so glad to see me and hear about my day," she said to the kitchen walls as she opened the refrigerator door. A crystal plate covered with a silver dome sat on the top shelf. Its coldness chilled her fingers as she carried it to the breakfast nook.

"Shrimp salad!" Her mouth watered. She touched her finger to the dressing, tasted its tangy tartness.

Changing her mind about eating in the breakfast nook, she carried her supper to her private bath, tossed a handful of gritty crystals into the tub and let them melt under a stream of hot water. Froth. Bubbles. She waited until the foamy water almost reached the rim of the tub before she pulled a tufted velvet stool to the tub side, placed her supper plate on it, then shed her clothes and stepped into the bath.

Heaven. This had to be as close to heaven as she'd ever get. So what if her parents preferred a concert to her company? So what if Glady and Herman were out? She relaxed, feeling the warm water against her skin, the cold shrimp in its tangy dressing against her tongue.

She smiled as she imagined Vonnie in her prim kitchen, sitting on a stright-backed chair and eating meat loaf and steamed veggies with her parents. But her smile faded as she imagined the conversation in the Morrison kitchen, conversation that probably centered on Vonnie and her day at school, as well as on her parents and their activities. She hated to admit that she was just a little jealous of Vonnie Morrison, the girl whom she felt sure was jealous of her. It was a crazy world!

Later that evening Monique drove to Vonnie's house. They went straight to Vonnie's room.

"Have you looked at the writing samples yet?"

"Haven't had time. Just now finished in the kitchen." Vonnie laid out the writing samples and snapped on the lamp before she opened the graphology book.

"Jason's first?" she asked. "Let's study overall effect."

"Quick-glance graphology? Why not." Monique studied the lines. "They don't go up. They don't slant down. But they're not absolutely level, either. They wander a bit within the line. Have you ever seen that before? What's it supposed to mean?"

Vonnie pointed to a paragraph in the book and a writing sample that showed script similar to the one they were examining. "You may have a person who's a little off balance."

"Jason? You're saying he's bonkers? Come on, Vonnie!"

"No." Vonnie laughed. "His writing just shows that he's changeable and maybe a little careless, but his small script reveals that he's an intellectual at heart."

"Not my sort of guy." Monique shoved the sheet aside. "Let's look at Ryan's writing." She reached for the sample. "Uphill all the way. What an optimist. Now he's more my type."

"Don't be too sure, Monique. His writing flows so strongly upward that it might indicate a person who's very ambitious and also one who tends to boast and brag and maybe even lie."

"A kiss-and-tell type?" Monique chewed on her lower lip, tasting the grape flavor of her lip gloss. "You're breaking my heart. You've shot both guys down at a glance."

"No way. Graphology isn't for shooting anyone down. So far we've only taken a quick overview. I'm sure we'll find things that'll counter these first indicators as we study the finer points of the writing."

"Let's see Mike's sample." Monique studied the third page. "Yuck! A pessimist. That's strange. I hadn't noticed that he acts all that pessimistic."

"He probably doesn't. Let's not make snap judgments. Maybe Mike's just moody. Or maybe he felt discouraged when he wrote this sample. It's a test paper with a C- on it. That could be discouraging. And look." Vonnie ran her finger under a line. "Sometimes a slight downward slant just means the a person doesn't waste time being unnecessarily enthusiastic."

"There are a lot of angles to graphology, aren't there?"

"Right."

Monique reached into her shoulder bag, feeling a lip gloss, then jabbing her finger against a nail file, before she pulled out a sheet of her own writing. "Look at this, Vonnie. Tell me what you see, okay?" She felt foolish sitting there waiting for Vonnie to analyze her. Why was she holding her breath?

Vonnie studied the sample for some time before she spoke. "Well, the upward slant could show optimism. The lines are widely spaced, and that shows a feeling of importance."

"We all need to feel important, don't we?"

"Right. There's nothing wrong with feeling important. Look at your capitals, Monique. They're large and open. That could mean that you're sometimes a bluffer."

"No fair looking right into my soul! Can't you come up with something good?"

"Sure. Your large letters indicate generosity and so does the forward angle of your writing as a whole. Your letters are spread apart and that also indicates a generous person, an intelligent person, a sensitive person."

"I wasn't fishing for flattery."

"I'm not dishing out flattery. I'm telling you what I see."

Monique kept her gaze on the page, but she considered Vonnie's words. Vonnie could have been negative about everything she saw in this writing, but she hadn't been. They had had lots of differences in the past, and although Vonnie knew she had the upper hand in this graphology business, she didn't take advantage of it. Monique admired her for that.

"Let's study some of your writing, Vonnie. How about it?"

"Sure. Why not?" Vonnie pulled a book report from her desk drawer, unfolded it and flattened it out on the desk.

"Level lines." Monique traced the first line of writing across the page with the tip of her ball-point. "They don't wander or waver within the line as Jason's did. What's that supposed to mean?''

"A strong determination to succeed," Vonnie said. "At least that's what the book says."

"You think that describes you?" Monique asked.

"Sure. I just wish I had a big goal in mind. You know—something important that I really want to pursue after high school. It would make all my determination more meaningful."

Monique pointed to the lines. "We both have the same large writing. But look at the slant of the letters. Mine lean to the right and yours lean slightly to the left, but on both samples the letters are widely spread within the word. You're generous."

"You're really catching on quickly," Vonnie said. "Remember that writing that slants slightly to the left indicates a shy, reserved person and writing that slants to the right shows a more outgoing personality."

"Our capital letters are quite different." Monique pointed to several of Vonnie's capitals. "Mine are large and open and yours are sort of pressed together as if you were short on space. If my capitals show a bluffer, then yours must show a person who avoids any sort of bragging."

"It could also show a shy person," Vonnie said.

"I don't think you're shy."

"I try to hide it. Maybe I've succeeded." Vonnie pointed to her signature and then to Monique's. "Did you notice that we both place a period after our names?"

"What's that tell you?" Monique asked.

"It means that we're concerned about what others think of us. And look at our big capital letters on our signatures."

"Big egos?" Monique asked.

"At first glance that might seem true, but look at the *i*'s later on in our names."

"They're very small."

"Right. According to the book that shows that we're both trying to cover up an inferiority complex."

Monique pretended to look on through the graphology book, but again she was thinking. Vonnie could have been mean about her analysis, but she hadn't been. She had been kind, and it surprised her that she and Vonnie had characteristics in common, especially the one about hiding an inferiority complex.

She hated to admit it, but she knew she felt inferior about her status in her family, and she tried to cover it up by bragging about her independence, her car. Deep down she also felt inferior about her poor grades. Did anyone guess that her show of not caring about grades was just a cover-up for her true feelings? She wondered what Vonnie felt inferior about. Her health? Did she really have a genuine illness that bugged her?

"What are you thinking, Monique? Are you ready to get on with analyzing more of these samples."

"Vonnie, I owe you an apology."

"What for?"

Monique tasted that rusty taste on the back of her tongue and knew then for sure that it came from nervousness rather than from fame. "For sounding off about your diabetes at the club meeting. I'm sorry I was so unfair."

"That's okay, Monique. No apology necessary. Lots of times it's hard for people who don't have diabetes to understand people who do. And sometimes it's hard for me to avoid envying kids with no health problems."

Feeling uncomfortable with so much apologizing, Monique stood. "I've got to go now, Vonnie. I guess I'm really getting hooked on graphology. I'm glad you introduced me to it.''

"Would you like to borrow this book? I have others.''

"Thanks a bunch.'' Monique slipped the book into her shoulder bag and left the house.

A week later Monique helped Vonnie collect follow-up writing samples from the play cast after a special morning rehearsal.

"Let's check them out, Vonnie. I can hardly wait.''

"Here?'' Vonnie asked. "Backstage?''

"Why not here? It's quiet and private. I'll go get you a lunch and we can work through the noon hour.''

"What about your own lunch?''

"I'm too excited to eat. We're giving three excerpts from the play during assembly at one o'clock, remember?''

"Couldn't forget it. I'm dying to see you onstage. Maybe we should wait until tonight to go over the writing samples.''

"Give me a break, Vonnie! I want to know if my personality has changed during this week of rehearsals. I want to know now.''

"Okay. I'll get my own lunch and be right back.''

Monique lined up the writing samples while Vonnie was gone. She studied her own first. Had she changed? Had her personality taken on facets that might be found in a city sophisticate?

"What do you think?''

Vonnie had returned so quietly that Monique jumped in surprise when she spoke.

"You're the expert,'' Monique said. "What do you see? Look at mine first.'' Monique could see slight differences in her writing, but very slight. The widely spaced lines were still there, as were the capitals and the small *i*'s.

"Look." Vonnie pointed. "No more circles dotting your *i*'s. That shows a new tendency to maturity. And look at the way you cross your *t*'s. Before the cross was formed in one stroke with the *t*-bar, and that indicated hastiness. This latest sample shows a cross about halfway up, and that indicates calmness. See, you have changed a bit as you've assumed a new character."

"So you've got the stuff you need for your article." Monique tried to imagine the finished piece in the school paper. Maybe she could get some cast pictures in, too, if she asked Miss Hunt.

"Cast onstage," Miss Baller called as a bell rang.

"Hey, I've got to go." Vonnie gathered up the samples.

Monique watched Vonnie leave, then she hurried to the girls' dressing room and began getting into costume. Slinky black dress. High-heeled sandals. Evening purse. The makeup girl put a towel around her neck and began applying foundation cream, and Monique closed her eyes and enjoyed all the attention.

"More eye shadow," someone said. "The spotlights will drink it up. Don't be afraid to apply plenty."

"Put on your own lip gloss, Monique," the makeup girl said. "You can do a better job than I can. Hurry. It's curtain time."

Monique had just applied the lip gloss when she heard Miss Baller's voice.

"Where's Jeff? He's supposed to be on left spotlight."

"He got sick this morning during math class," Jason said.

"Sick!" Miss Baller shouted the word.

"I can find someone to run the spot," Monique said.

"Who?" Miss Baller asked. "We need someone who knows what he's doing."

"Vonnie Morrison," Monique said. "I know right where she's sitting. She did lighting for a play back in Kansas."

"Get her up in the left balcony, then," Miss Baller said. "She'll have to do. Hurry. It's curtain time."

Although she hated to reveal her costume offstage, Monique hurried out front to the senior section and motioned to Vonnie. "Emergency, Vonnie. Can you run the left spot for us?"

"Right now?"

"Of course right now." Monique grabbed Vonnie's wrist and pulled her toward the balcony stairs. "You said you'd done it before. Jeff's absent and we need you."

"Do you have a play book?"

"No. You don't need one. Just follow the actor who's on left stage. Keep that person in the spotlight."

"But ... but ..."

"You can handle it, Vonnie. I'm on stage left a lot. Just keep me in the spotlight."

Monique gave Vonnie a quick introduction to the head of the lighting crew, then hurried backstage. What if she'd made a mistake? She and Vonnie had gotten along much better lately, but maybe she had been a fool to put Vonnie in a position that could make or break her performance.

Eight

The balcony was hot and Vonnie felt perspiration dampen her forehead as she listened to the boy in charge of lights explain the use of the spot. Why had she gotten into this? But how could she have said no? She owed Monique one.

"Vonnie," Lora called, joining her. "What are you doing up here? I thought we were going to sit together downstairs."

"I'm in charge of this spotlight. It's an emergency. The regular guy went home sick without telling Miss Baller." She tasted salt as she licked her upper lip, and she paused long enough to wipe her face with a tissue.

"It's like a furnace up here, but I'll keep you company." Lora sat down beside the spotlight.

"Thanks. I can use some moral support." Vonnie snapped the spot on and then off to be sure it was working. "I just couldn't turn Monique down. She was in a real panic."

"Yeah," Lora said. "Monique has a hard time surviving without a spotlight whether she's onstage or off."

"Ease up, Lora. She's really doing a good job in the play."

"Monique only helped you get writing samples because she wanted to see her name in the paper. Wake up, Vonnie. She's using you."

"Maybe I was using her. There are two ways to look at it. We both got what we wanted."

The roaring tide of voices ebbed as the president of the student body walked to stage center. The sound system squealed a couple of times, but the sound crew got it under control quickly.

"And now we bring you...*City Symphony*. Curtain, please!"

The curtain pulleys whispered, and the velvet panels slowly parted to reveal Monique and Tish in a theater scene. Vonnie snapped on the spotlight, focusing it carefully on Monique as she said her lines and then on Tish as she took her place.

"Doesn't she look absolutely neat?" Vonnie whispered to Lora. "Watch how she holds herself. Notice the way she moves. That dress makes her look at least twenty. Maybe even twenty-one." Vonnie shifted the light quickly, focusing it carefully.

"Monique's not projecting her voice," Lora said. "I missed part of her last line. Tish comes across much more clearly."

Vonnie stopped whispering and concentrated on keeping the spotlight trained on whichever actor was speaking, usually Monique. She had a lot of lines.

When the first excerpt ended, the curtain closed briefly, then as soon as the set had been rearranged, the actors transported the audience to a café scene, and finally, in the last excerpt, to a sophisticated apartment setting.

"I think they could use more practice," Lora said as the curtain closed and the audience began clapping.

"It's only normal for them to be nervous," Vonnie said. "That's what this performance was for—to help the cast get used to a live audience."

"I suppose so." Lora stood. "Let's get back downstairs. I'm dying of the heat."

"I admire Monique's confidence." Vonnie sighed. "She's really into her character."

"Maybe she didn't have to do all that much acting," Lora said. "Baller knows it pays to cast to type."

"Monique's not as sophisticated as she lets on," Vonnie said as they walked down the stairs into cooler air.

"I thought you hated Monique, Vonnie. A few days ago you were eating lunch at home to avoid her. We all just sort of tolerate her because of Randy, because he's part of the gang. How come you're sticking up for her all of a sudden?"

"I've been studying samples of her handwriting. The beneath-the-surface Monique is a lot different from the Monique she shows to the world."

"But we're stuck with the Monique she shows to the world. Unfortunately."

"She's really not all that bad, Lora."

"She's brainwashed you."

"No I tell you, her writing has given me some fresh insights. She worries about what others think of her more than you'd dream."

"I can't imagine her caring about what I think of her. She makes it clear she thinks I live in the past lane."

"She's also oversensitive to criticism, and she's over-eager to be liked. I see all those things in her writing."

"Did you tell her so?"

"I've told her some of it. But not all."

"Here she comes," Lora said. "Color me gone."

Before Vonnie could protest, Lora skinned through an empty row of seats and took a side exit.

"Lora, wait," Vonnie called, but Lora didn't return. It was too late to chase after her; Monique was heading toward her, her smile impaling Vonnie to the spot.

"What did you think, Vonnie? How did I do?"

"You were wonderful, Monique. Really! Miss Baller couldn't have chosen a better lead." Vonnie breathed in the fragrance of gardenia perfume as she reached out to touch the silky fabric in Monique's black dress. "Your hair, Monique. It was perfect." Vonnie looked at Monique's hair wistfully. "I may try letting mine grow."

"Vonnie, you were great on the lights. Really super. Come backstage with me until I change and I'll drive you home."

"Okay." Why not? Lora had ditched her, Bob was nowhere in sight, and school had been dismissed early for a teachers' meeting.

By the time she and Monique reached the dressing room, the other girls had left, and only the smell of greasepaint and cologne remained. Theater. This is how theater smells, Vonnie thought. Glamorous. Exciting. She felt out of place in her denim and madras as she sat on a three-legged stool to wait while Monique slathered her face in pink cleansing cream.

"I've made a decision, Vonnie." Monique reached for a tissue. "I haven't told another soul, but I've decided on a career. I'm going to be an actress. I'm going to work and study and practice and...and if you laugh, I'll throttle you."

"I'm not laughing. You did a supergreat job out there this afternoon. Acting could be your big thing."

"I really think it could," Monique agreed. "I read lots of movie mags, and you'd be surprised how many actors got their start on a high school stage. I may enroll in some voice lessons, some dancing lessons, some acting lessons."

"Can you handle all that and school, too?"

"Who cares about school?" Monique began applying her regular makeup. "What we're talking here is career. The big time. Theater audiences don't care about grades. They care about important things like looks and clothes. They're interested in who you're dating or who you're living with. It's a different world out there, Vonnie, and I'm on my way."

"Go for it, Monique. There's no reason you can't be whatever you want to be."

Vonnie said little more on the ride home in Monique's Camaro. She didn't have to. She couldn't have. Monique chattered on and on about her new career. Vonnie didn't laugh. Monique's enthusiasm carried Vonnie along with it until they reached her house.

After the Camaro pulled away, Vonnie felt slightly deflated as she found herself left with her handwriting samples and the knowledge that she was expected to produce an article for *The Iconoclast*. Writing didn't seem nearly as much fun or as glamorous as acting, especially now that she had to get to work on her article.

Vonnie stayed up that night, working on her article until her mother tapped on her door.

"Know what time it is, Von? Can't whatever you're doing wait until tomorrow?"

"It's the article for the paper, Mom, and it's due tomorrow. But I'm about finished with it. Want to read it?"

"Sure." The bed creaked as her mother sat on the edge of the mattress and read the piece, nodding her approval as she turned the pages. "Very good. Miss Hunt should be pleased."

"I hope so."

"Vonnie..." Her mother hesitated before continuing. "Vonnie, maybe you should ease up a little."

"Ease up? Why? What do you mean?"

Her mother stood. "It's just that you never seem to have time to have any fun. You're always either studying or worrying about the graphology club or... or now working and worrying about this article."

"But, Mom, I like doing all those things. I know I fuss around about them, but basically, I like what I'm doing."

"I know you do." Her mother gave her a hug. "Forget I said anything."

As soon as her mother left, Vonnie snapped off her light and snuggled into the cool sheets. In some ways she wished she were more like Monique, carefree and fun loving, but in other ways she was quite happy to be ordinary Vonnie Morrison.

On Wednesday Miss Hunt okayed Vonnie's article. On Friday the student body gave it their approval. Vonnie heard kids she didn't even know talking about the article between classes, trying to analyze their own or someone else's handwriting. Strangers spoke to her in the halls, sometimes stopping to ask questions. And, best of all, a dozen more kids signed up for the graphology club.

"Neat article, Vonnie," Bob said when the gang met in the lunch room. "May I have your autograph?"

"You're kidding."

"No way." Bob spread the paper out on the table. "Just sign right below your byline."

Vonnie signed Bob's paper, feeling very self-conscious, yet very pleased as she listened to the pen glide over the sheet. Never before had anyone ever asked for her autograph.

"Miss Hunt will be trying to snag you into journalism classes next semester," Bob said. "Better be prepared for her."

"It might not be a bad idea," Vonnie said. "I really liked writing the article. Maybe I'd be smart to try journalism as an elective."

"Better let me show you how to use a computer," Bob said. "You may be needing it."

"So far the typewriter's plenty speedy enough." Vonnie casually took a sip of milk, but she basked in all the compliments the kids were handing out.

"Did you see my handwriting in the paper?" Arriving late, Monique plunked her tray onto the table and pulled out her chair with a flourish. "It shows I'm very deep into my stage role."

"Is a stage roll anything like a jelly roll?" Dick made slurping sounds with his milk straw. "Jelly rolls are my favorites."

"Get serious, Dick." Tish punched him playfully on the arm. "I think Monique's very good in the play, and I think Vonnie's article was supergreat publicity for the whole cast. We should have a sold-out house for all three evening performances."

"Did you see how many more kids have signed up for graphology club?" Cass asked. "At least a dozen."

"Nice going, Vonnie," Randy said, joining the group and pulling up a chair beside Monique. "You're really going to make that club catch on. Lots of new organizations are past history after the first meeting, but not this one."

"Did you see my handwriting in the paper, Randy?" Monique asked. "It shows that I'm deep into my stage character. Do you agree?"

"I think what we have here is a broken record," Dick said.

"Sure, I saw your writing," Randy said, ignoring Dick's remark. "Everyone saw it." He smiled at Vonnie. "Great job, Von. You've written a state-of-the-art article."

"Anyone can write a super article given super subject matter," Monique said. "But it takes real ability to submerge your own personality and to project a new one from the stage."

"And you heard it from Monique Wagar first," Dick said. "Her middle initial, M, stands for Modesty."

"Lay off, Dick," Cass said. "You're being V.D."

"Right," Lora said. "Besides, we've got a problem here. Where are we going to hold the next club meeting? If a dozen more kids join, we may need to find a bigger meeting place."

Vonnie glared at Lora. Didn't she know that she wanted to hold the meeting at her house. She certainly didn't want to hold it at the school. That might make it seem too much like just another class.

"I can handle the crowd at my house," Vonnie said. "We can spread out to the patio if the inside gets overcrowded."

"The patio?" Lora asked. "In November? It's too cold."

"It's been warm enough the past few evenings," Vonnie pointed out. "It was almost eighty in the early part of the evening."

"Unseasonably warm." Dick slurped his milk again. "That's what the news announcer calls it. He means it's something you can't depend on."

"No problem, kids," Monique said. "We can have the meeting at my house. My folks don't watch me like a hawk. They give me lots of freedom and they want me to invite friends in whenever I please. We'd have the place to ourselves except for Glady and Herman who would make and serve the refreshments."

"What a switch!" Cass glared at Monique. "Last time you and Tish didn't even come to the meeting, at least not to all of it. And as I remember it you weren't all that entranced with graphology—or refreshments. Why the big change?"

"I've changed my mind about the subject, Cassie." Monique gave her a phony smile. "A woman's got a right to change her mind, you know, especially an actress. Actresses are noted for changing their minds."

"What good would it do to meet at your house?" Lora asked Monique. "You've got a big patio, true, but it's still outside. Maybe we should plan to meet at the school."

"Bad thinking," Bob said. "Nobody wants to go back to school at night!"

"Not so," Tish said. "I think going back for play practice has been a gas."

"That's different," Lora said. "You need the stage."

"I have a big house," Monique said. "We can meet inside if it's a cool evening, or we can meet on the patio if it's a warm evening. We can choose the best of two worlds. And of course we'd be able to swim in the heated pool after the meeting's over and we're into refreshments. Everyone bring your suits."

Vonnie's fork clattered against her plate. How dared Monique act as if a change of meeting place was all decided! A burning surge of heat rose from her stomach to her neck to her face. That Monique! She was just assuming that the group would fall in with her plans. Bring your suits, indeed! How could she have thought even for a minute that Monique was her friend? Next thing they knew Monique would be trying to claim that the graphology club was all her idea in the first place, sort of a Super Seniors club featuring graphology instead of shoplifting.

Lora had been right. Monique had used her. But she wasn't going to let her get away with it.

"We'll go ahead and hold the meeting at my house," Vonnie said in a firm voice. "We'll find room. No problem."

Vonnie welcomed the sound of the afternoon bell and hurried to class before any more could be said about the club meeting. She had definitely called Monique's bluff.

That afternoon after school Bob walked home with her as he usually did on Fridays, and they made plans for the evening.

"Rod's playing with a group at Tut's Tomb out near the Astrodome tonight," Bob said. "The gang's going to hang out there. Can Lora and I pick you up around eight?"

"Sure. Sounds neat. I've never heard Rod play anyplace except at school."

"Me either. Lora has, though. Several times. She says the group's cool."

The three of them sat in the front seat that night as they drove to Tut's Tomb. Waste flares at the refineries lit the sky to their left once they drove from the city, and the smell of oil hung in the soft night air that wafted through the open windows.

"There it is up ahead." Lora pointed. "Tut's Tomb."

"Funky name," Bob said.

"At least it's one a person remembers," Lora said. "Rod says the name attracts business because people think they've heard lots about the place before."

Vonnie eyed the windowless stucco building that sat at the front of a vast parking lot. Buff colored. Brown trim decorated with gold death masks. She smelled hot grease and the fragrance of garlic even before Bob opened the door.

"Over here." Randy waved and called to them from where he and Monique were sitting at a large table directly in front of the band. Bob pulled out chairs for Vonnie and Lora, then sat between them.

"Hi, gang," Rod called from his seat at the electric piano. "Let's hear some requests. We've got a big book and if we know your favorite tune, we'll be glad to play it."

"'Missin' You,'" Lora called quickly.

Rod winked at her. "You got it."

Vonnie felt the floorboards vibrating as the group began to play. Piano. Bass guitar. Drums. Saxophone. With the sound system cranked up, it sounded like forty players instead of only four.

As soon as the number ended, Lora called out another request. "'Dreamboat.'"

"Hey, look who's joining us," Monique said. "Tish! Chet! Over here."

Chet sat on the other side of Vonnie just as the group stopped playing. After he and Tish had ordered burgers and fries, he turned to Vonnie.

"Neat place."

"Yeah. It is. Good group playing, too. Rod's lucky to be working gigs with them."

"Maybe they're lucky to be working with Rod," Lora said. "It could work both ways."

"And I'm lucky to have a cousin to show me around," Chet said.

"Cousin!" Dick said. "You're kidding. We thought Tish had a new boyfriend."

"Dick!" Cass said reproachfully.

"Well, it's the truth, isn't it? This is the first time I've heard anything about a cousin."

"Maybe some of us did think Chet was Tish's boyfriend," Cass said. "But..."

"I thought I told you Chet was my cousin," Tish said. "I've had my mind so much on the play that I might have forgotten, but it doesn't matter. Chet and I are friends, as well as cousins."

Vonnie felt her heart sink. She had thought it strange that Tish had gone right on flirting with Bob even after Chet had made the scene, but why should she worry! Bob had invited her here tonight, hadn't he? No sweat!

At intermission Rod joined the gang at the table, taking his place beside Lora and ordering pizza for the two of them.

"You got a great sound, man," Dick said.

"Yeah," Cass agreed. "Really great."

"Rod?" Monique said. "Is there a chance this group would play a private party?"

"Sure." Rod flexed his fingers as if they were tired. "That's what we're in business for, to play gigs. You throwing a party?"

"Nothing big," Monique said. "Maybe while we're having refreshments after the graphology club meeting the group could set up around our pool and play for an hour or so."

"Who's picking up the tab?" Rod asked.

"My daddy would pay," Monique said. "No problem there."

"Monique," Vonnie said. "The meeting's going to be at my house, not yours."

"We'll see," Monique said, giving Vonnie a patronizing smile.

"If you want The Greasy Cans to play, you better sign a contract with us. That's the way we work."

"My dad would have to sign it," Monique said. "I'd have to talk with him first, of course. But, gang, I've got a new idea for the club."

"Give," Cass said. "Tell all."

Vonnie felt every muscle tighten, and she thought she might fly into pieces if Monique even came close to telling all.

"At the next meeting, I'm going to come up with lots of samples of teachers' writing."

"How?" Rod asked.

"Easy," Monique said. "Every kid in school has some teacher's writing on his old assignment papers. I'll just collect a bunch and we'll be ready to go. We can analyze them and then guess which teacher the writing belongs to. It'd be a gas."

"Neat idea," Randy said. "Very neat."

"Uptown," Tish agreed and looked at Bob for further confirmation.

Vonnie clenched her fists under the table when she saw Bob nod in agreement with Tish.

"And I've got another idea," Monique said. "Everyone of us has some person we secretly admire. It may be someone we're close to every day, or it may be a special secret someone we admire from a distance and would like to know better."

"Get to the point," Dick said.

"So let's each of us get a writing sample from a person we admire and practice analyzing it at the club meeting. You can keep the name of your chosen person top secret. It'll just be between you and the writing sample."

"Sounds great," Tish said.

"Depends on whom you admire," Rod said, looking at Lora thoughtfully.

"So it's settled," Monique said. "The club's going to meet at my house. We'll analyze teachers' writing, a secret would-be friend's writing, and Rod's group will play during refreshment time around the pool."

"The club meeting will be held at my house," Vonnie said. "I insist." She leaned forward so everyone could see and hear her.

"Hey," Dick said. "The only fair way to decide this is to take a vote. How many want to go to Monique's place?"

Vonnie's neck itched from heat and anger as she saw every hand go up except hers and Lora's. She started to get up, but Bob pulled her back into her chair.

"Come on, Vonnie," he whispered. "Be cool."

"No," Vonnie whispered back. "Monique's being a nerd, and I'm not going to let her get away with it."

"Why does it matter so much where the meeting's held?" Bob asked. "I think you're just green-eyed because Monique is coming up with such good ideas."

Vonnie stood. This was the second time Bob had come right out and accused her of being jealous of Monique. How could he!

"I don't feel well, Bob," Vonnie said, turning from the table. "I'm going to call my dad to come get me."

"You're faking it, Vonnie," Bob whispered. "Monique's right about you. Sometimes you fake it when things don't go your way."

Enough! Too much! Vonnie left the table and headed for the public phone near the door. When she heard footsteps behind her, she thought they were Bob's, and she was half ready to listen to an apology.

Chet's voice surprised her.

"Let me take you home, Vonnie. I've made enough of this scene for tonight."

"Thanks, Chet, but I'll call my dad. He won't mind coming for me." The quarter felt cold to her fingers as she dropped it in the coin slot. She dialed and listened while the phone rang ten times. Reluctantly, she replaced the receiver and retrieved her quarter.

"Come on," Chet urged. "I'll drive you home. I think it's time we got better acquainted."

Vonnie wanted to refuse. Of all times for her parents to be out! If she went with Chet, Bob would be sure to take Tish home.

But she couldn't just walk back to the table and tell Bob she suddenly felt better. Turning to Chet, she smiled.

"Thanks for the offer, Chet. Let's go."

Nine

On Monday morning a mist formed on the windows of the Camaro as Monique drove it from the cool garage into the warm morning air. The windshield wipers swished smoothly for a few moments before they began to drag against dry glass. Monique frowned. This was November. Why wasn't it cooler? Didn't Texas know about fall and winter?

If the temperature stayed up, Vonnie would be justified in insisting that the club meeting be at her house. On second thought Monique smiled to herself, knowing it would do Vonnie no good to insist now. The kids had voted. They had voted for her. Leaning back against the leather seat cushion, she hummed along with the Springsteen tune blaring from the radio as the Camaro glided smoothly along the busy street.

She stopped by Randy's house on her way to school, tooted the horn once, then when Randy was on the seat beside her she deliberately drove out of her way toward Piney Glen where she know Vonnie and Lora would be walking.

"What's up?" Randy asked. "Why are you going this way? Discovered a quicker route?"

Monique looked at him from under her heavy fringe of lashes. "I was just curious to know if Vonnie has recovered from her sudden illness. Thought we'd drive by her house and see if she's able to be out and about."

Dropping his armload of books onto the floor of the car, Randy looked at Monique. "I suppose you think she was faking it Friday night, right?"

"You've got it."

"I tell you her health problems are for real. There's no question in my mind. None at all."

"A few days ago I might have believed you. A few days ago I thought Vonnie and I might be friends, but Friday night put our relationship back on square one."

"Why?"

"There are lots of questions in my mind about Vonnie." Monique signaled for a left turn. "I think she used me to help with her article. I also think she faked illness because she just couldn't deal with not having the club meeting at her house. She's so deeply weird. What difference can the location of the meeting make?"

"Maybe she feels more comfortable at her own house. I can understand that."

"Why do you always stick up for her!" Her knuckles grew white on the steering wheel. "I think she's jealous and petty and . . . I don't really like her at all."

"Maybe you haven't really tried to understand her."

"I've tried. Really tried. I wish she was out of my space. In spite of everything you've said, I just don't like her and I don't know what the gang sees in her."

"Hold it, Monique. You're being unfair. Vonnie's a good kid. She's serious about school, but she goes for a good time as quick as anyone else."

"Guess last Friday just wasn't one of her good-time nights. She really threw a damper on the party. The kids forgot all about listening to Rod's group."

"Hardly. The music was too loud to forget. My ears are still ringing."

"I'll bet Rod wishes she had stayed at home. He was supposed to be the star of the evening, at least from his friends' point of view."

"Everybody in the gang likes Vonnie, Monique. I'll bet you can't find jealousy or pettiness indicated in her handwriting."

"You're not really going to take handwriting analysis all that seriously, are you?"

"I'm not sure. I don't know enough about it yet. But I don't think Vonnie's petty."

Monique braked at a stoplight. "I've taken a careful look at her writing."

"But you don't know how to analyze it."

"Sure I do. I've been reading a handbook on the subject. It showed examples of all sorts of writing. I spent a lot of time this past weekend studying them."

"Where'd you get the book?"

"Vonnie lent it to me."

"Would a petty person lend a competitor ammunition to use against her?"

"This one did. Maybe that shows she's not too smart a competitor." Monique eased the car on through the intersection. "Why are we wasting time arguing about Vonnie? She's off the wall."

"You've been putting in a lot of time studying her writing, haven't you?"

"Of course. Why not? That's the point of this wonderful science of graphology, isn't it? To learn more about one's friends and one's . . . enemies."

"What did you learn? Honestly now, Monique. What did you see in Vonnie's writing?"

Monique hesitated, then shrugged. She had tried to change the subject, but it hadn't worked. She could lie a little. But no. She might lie to some people, but not to Randy.

"Vonnie's writing indicated calmness and honesty and generosity with quite a bit of caution and shyness and determination thrown in for good measure, but I'll admit I may have misinterpreted the book. I really don't find those characteristics in her actual personality. At least not consistently."

"What's that supposed to mean?"

"Vonnie and I were getting on a lot better a few days ago. She invited me to her house. I drove her here and there. It was sort of neat, and I really can't understand what happened to spoil it. But I can't stand an on-again, off-again friend. I really need to know how I rate with people."

"Maybe you haven't really tried to find the characteristics her writing shows. You two just got off on the wrong foot right from the start."

"Be real, Randy. You can't actually learn to know a person through his writing. And I've tried to understand Vonnie. I've tried to understand her ever since the first day we met at school and she was assigned to show me the ropes. What a joke. I could show her a thing or two any day of the week. She's a mystery, but I'm not sure she's a mystery that's worth trying to figure out."

"Then why are you suddenly so interested in the graphology club? You must think there's some truth in graphology or you wouldn't have been so insistent on having the meeting at your house."

"I was just doing everyone a big favor by offering my patio and pool. I was being generous." Monique flung her hair over her shoulder. "Generosity shows up in my writing. Even Vonnie said so. She found three different things that indicated a generous person."

"Nobody's saying you aren't generous."

"I want everyone to have fun, and it's hard to have fun when there're too many kids crammed into a small house like Vonnie's."

"I think you intentionally hurt her feelings."

"Sure I did. And that's why she flounced off in such a huff Friday night. Hurt feelings. It had nothing at all to do with insulin or diabetes."

"You can't say that for sure."

"Why are you sticking up for her so, Randy? It bugs me. You were there. You heard the kids vote to come to my house for the meeting. If Vonnie hadn't been so stubborn she wouldn't have had her feelings hurt."

"But..."

"There they are, Randy. Lora and Vonnie. Prepare yourself to watch my generosity in action." Monique tooted the horn, lowered the window and slowed down as she pulled into the left lane. "Want a ride?"

Vonnie and Lora both looked up, surprised.

"Sure thing." Lora hurried to the car and opened the door. "You saved my life. My arms were about to break from carrying all this homework."

"Come on, Vonnie," Monique called.

"I forgot one of my books," Vonnie said, turning back toward her house. "You go on ahead. I'll go home for it. Catch you later."

"Oh, come on, Vonnie." Monique eased the car forward a few inches. "What difference does a book make? You can borrow one from somebody. Or you can do without it for a day. Who'll notice? No big deal.''

A driver pulled up behind Monique, honked his horn and Monique drove on toward school. Vonnie Morrison had some nerve. Few people ever turned down a ride in the Camaro.

"Take a right and drive around the block," Randy said, turning to check the traffic behind them. "We can pick her up in front of her house after she gets her book."

"No way," Monique said. "She had her chance. I'm not into being snubbed. Can't you see how she's treating me! You expect me to take that!"

"She didn't snub you," Lora said. "She just forgot her book."

"You're dipping into the world of paranoia," Randy said.

"Do you believe everything that girl says?" Monique snorted. "Vonnie Morrison has probably never forgotten a schoolbook in her whole life."

"Until this morning," Lora said.

"I consider a refusal to ride with me a snub, and I hate it. And I don't understand both of you turning on me like this. I went out of my way to help Vonnie get writing samples for her article and you know it. Now that she has them and has used them to promote Vonnie Morrison, she's treating me like dirt, but you two refuse to admit it."

"Cool it, Monique," Lora said. "You helped her get the samples because one of them was yours and you wanted to see your name in the paper. You're lucky she let you help her."

"What a way to start Monday morning." Randy scooped his books from the floor. "How did I get caught in the middle of all this crazy arguing!"

"If you feel so caught, maybe you'd like to walk the rest of the way." Monique braked the car, and to her surprise Randy got out, slammed the door and headed toward school without a backward glance.

"Some friend!" Monique peeled out, burning rubber. "Some really true friend. I'll never speak to him again. Never."

Lora giggled.

"What's so funny?"

Lora giggled again. "It's just that with you driving and me sitting in the back seat, you look as if you're my chauffeur or something. I love it."

"Live it up," Monique said. "Enjoy. You may never have another chance." She wheeled into the school parking lot, slammed on the brakes and left the car quickly, not waiting to see whether Lora was coming with her. Vonnie. Randy. Lora. Everyone was turning against her, even laughing at her. Vonnie Morrison would pay for this.

Monique hurried inside the schoolhouse and stopped in front of the bulletin board. Groping in her shoulder bag, she was searching for a pen when Dick approached.

"Got a problem?" he asked.

Monique's first instinct was to keep looking at the bulletin board and ignore Dick. Cass was the only person she knew who really enjoyed seeing him or being seen with him. On the other hand, maybe he could help her.

"Got a pen, Dick? I need to change the address of the club meeting to my place so the new kids won't waste time going to the wrong house."

Dick pulled a felt-tip pen from the pocket of his black leather jacket. "Here you go. This's better than a ball-point, and red will show up better than black."

Taking the felt-tip, Monique crossed out Vonnie's address and wrote in her own. She had thought Dick would go on his way, but instead he followed her to every bulletin board in the school, running his hand over his crazy haircut as he stood and watched her make the changes.

"How about my pen?" Dick held out his hand when Monique was finished.

"Of course, Dick." She gave him a disdainful smile. "It must be quite valuable."

"A guy can lose a lot of pens this way," Dick said.

"We wouldn't want that to happen, now would we?" Monique returned the felt-tip, leaving it uncapped and smiling as red ink smeared on his fingers.

"Dick," Cass called to him. "I've been looking everywhere for you. Where have you been? You were supposed to meet me at the front door ten minutes ago."

"I've been helping Monique," Dick said in his usual loud voice. "She forgot to bring a pen."

Monique gritted her teeth as passersby turned to look at them. She hoped she didn't look like the type who'd be seeking Dick Randall's company.

Monday. She hated Mondays. Morning classes dragged by, and she was tempted to skip lunch and go home for the day, but to her surprise Randy was waiting at her locker. Any other time she would really have made him pay for walking out on her that morning. She would have demanded an apology, or she would have refused to speak to him, but right now she had to admit she was glad to see him.

"Going to lunch?" Randy asked.

"Lunch? Just like that? No apology or anything?" Monique kept her voice haughty as she held her head high.

"No apology. I've got nothing to apologize for. In fact, you might consider giving me an apology."

"For what?"

"Forget that I mentioned it. Are you or are you not going to lunch?"

"I'm going. In just a minute." She couldn't let him off scot-free, and she knew how he hated being at the end of the lunch line. "I have to comb my hair." She headed for the rest room, taking her time as she went. "Wait for me, okay?"

Randy looked at his watch. "Okay."

She smiled as she saw him eyeing the kids lining up to have lunch tickets punched. It would serve him right to have to wait. Once the rest room door had closed behind her, she pulled a brush from her bag and brushed her hair one hundred slow strokes. Then she sprayed it smooth. Washing her hands killed another few minutes, as did applying a little perfume. When she emerged from the rest room, the lunch line reached halfway down the hall.

"Smells like pizza today," Monique said as if she had nothing in the world more important to do than wait to get into the cafeteria.

They were so late in heading to their places that most of the gang had already finished eating and were munching apples or cookies.

"Hey, look." Monique nudged Randy as they approached their table. "There've been some changes made. Tish and Bob are sitting at one end of the table, and Vonnie and Chet seem to be an item at the opposite end. How about that?"

"Could be accidental," Randy said.

"Dream on, Randy. Tish has been waiting for this day almost since school started last fall. She told me so at play practice. She's been bonkers over Bob for ages."

Monique and Randy sat down, and Monique was biting into her pizza when Lora spoke up.

"Have you heard the big news about Vonnie, Monique?"

"The only big news I've heard is that she forgot her textbook this morning."

"Miss Hunt called her to the journalism room before first class and asked her to write another article for the school paper." Lora turned to Vonnie. "What will you write about this next time?"

"More about graphology," Vonnie said. "That's what she says the kids want. She said something about starting a regular column, but I don't know if I could find enough time to do that."

"You could just analyze someone's writing for each issue," Bob said.

"Or you could write a column on every letter in the alphabet," Cass said. "That'd make twenty-six quick columns."

"There aren't that many weeks left in the school year," Monique said. "Bad idea. Anyway, the kids will soon get tired of reading about graphology. Too trendy. The craze will pass, just like any other fad."

Monique took another bite of pizza before she noticed Vonnie glaring at her.

"Feeling sick again?" Monique asked with mock seriousness. "You had us all scared to death Friday night."

"I was feeling just fine until I saw the bulletin boards," Vonnie said.

"The bulletin boards?" Monique kept her voice light and gave Vonnie her wide-eyed innocent look.

"You know what I mean," Vonnie said. "The changed address on the posters. I took masking tape and covered the mess you made before I penned in my address again."

"But, Vonnie, the gang voted. They want to come to my house. I'm the one who's collected the teachers' writing samples. I'm the one who came up with the idea of analyzing the writing of a secret friend. Don't be an old stick about this. You'll only spoil everyone's fun."

"Monique," Vonnie began. "My friends asked me to lead this club and that's what I'm going to do. You're not going to take over. I'll lead the meeting only if it's at my house."

"That's really no big threat, Vonnie," Monique said. "I've studied the graphology book all weekend. I've practically *memorized* it. I know as much about this pseudoscience as you do, and I can easily lead the discussion."

Nobody at the table spoke. Some of the gang looked at Monique and some of them looked at Vonnie. Monique felt as if she and her friends were inside a bubble of silence while noise raged all around them. She waited for Vonnie to say something, but to her surprise, Bob broke the silence.

"Listen up, gang. I don't know why we've gotten so bent out of shape over this club meeting. It's just that, a meeting. No really big deal. Remember how we felt a while back? We were excited about learning to know what our writing might reveal."

"Yeah," Cass said. "And I'm still interested."

The group muttered in agreement.

"So if we're all still interested," Bob said, "let's stop the arguing about a meeting place. Vonnie's our leader. We chose her. I don't know about the rest of you, but I'm going to her house for the meeting."

Another bubble of silence encased the group, then it burst as one by one the kids began to side with Bob. Monique could hardly believe it was happening. Vonnie had squelched the Super Seniors, and now this!

"I'll see you at your house tomorrow, Vonnie," Lora said. "You can count on it."

"Me too," Rod said. "Where Lora goes, I go."

"I'll be there, too," Cass agreed. "And so will Dick, won't you, Dick?"

"If you say so," Dick said.

"What about you, Tish?" Lora asked. "And Chet?"

"I'll be there," Tish said.

"Count me present," Chet agreed. "Vonnie's house at seven o'clock, right?"

"Right," Bob said

"Monique?" Lora faced Monique. "What about you? We want you to come. Will you be there?"

"What will you do if I refuse? Just what will you do? I can take all the new kids with me to my house if I decide to. I could offer transportation in the Camaro, fun in the pool, special refreshments."

"But are you sure that's what you really want to do?" Lora asked.

"How about it, Randy?" Monique asked. "I'll let you decide."

"I'm meeting at Vonnie's with the rest of the gang. Why don't I pick you up? If we have a strong club, we're going to have to work together."

"Right," Bob said. "Everyone. Be a sport, Monique. Shake the bugs out of your program and show us your cooperative mode."

"On one condition." Monique knew she was in no real position to be making conditions, but she tried, anyway. "I'll attend the meeting at Vonnie's if we go on with my planned activities, analyzing teachers' writing, working with the secret friend idea. And just to show you what a good sport I am, I'll make enough copies of the writing samples to pass out one to every person."

"How about it, kids?" Bob asked. "Monique's offering bells and whistles. Shall we accept?"

"Right," several voices called out.

"Is it okay with you, Vonnie?" Bob asked. "The content of the meeting, I mean."

Monique looked directly at Vonnie, waiting for her answer. Did she just imagine it, or had Vonnie grown pale? If Vonnie balked at this point, she didn't know what she could do to save face.

"It's fine with me," Vonnie said.

The group broke up and everyone headed for the hallway and the lockers. Monique felt a strong sense of being both a winner and a loser, and she held back from the others, threading her way slowly between the cafeteria tables, not wanting to talk to anyone just then. Not even Randy. Especially not Randy. She walked alone for a few moments before she noticed Vonnie just ahead of her.

It wasn't until Vonnie slumped into a chair that Monique realized something was wrong. Or was it? Maybe Vonnie was faking it again.

Ten

A burning anger at Monique helped propel Vonnie toward the lunchroom exit. She felt hot and cold at the same time, and she knew she had all but made a fool of herself over the location of the club meeting both last Friday and again today. Why had she let it take over her life? She tried to hurry to her afternoon classes, but the door seemed so far away. And what had happened to the doorframe? It looked twenty feet wide at the top yet very narrow at the bottom. She might have trouble easing through it.

Then suddenly she realized that the sensation of heat and cold, the visual distortions were insulin related. Why hadn't she been more alert! Quick! She tried to speak, but she couldn't. She barely had enough strength to sink into a chair.

"Lora? Bob?" In her mind the words were shouts, but in reality they were mere whispers. She groped in her shoulder bag for some lemon drops.

"Monique," Randy called. "Move it. We're going to be late."

Vonnie heard Randy's voice coming from a great distance, then she saw Monique, towering above her like a great blond giant. She clutched Monique's hand.

"Vonnie, are you okay?" Monique stared at her, glanced in Randy's direction as if she might join him as he left the lunchroom, then once more turned her attention back to Vonnie.

"Vonnie? You okay? Vonnie, what's the matter? Your eyes. They're rolling and . . ."

"Candy," Vonnie whispered, then felt herself slumping forward in her chair. "Need candy."

"Where is it?" Monique shook Vonnie's shoulder. "Answer me, Vonnie."

When Vonnie didn't answer, Monique dumped the contents of Vonnie's bag onto the table and grabbed a lemon drop from the white sack that had almost fallen on the floor. Quickly she held it to Vonnie's lips and pushed it into her mouth.

"Juice," Vonnie muttered as she sucked on the candy.

Monique grabbed Vonnie's billfold and hurried to the vending machine beside the lunchroom door. As Vonnie forced her eyes open to watch, Monique's body seemed to waver just above the floor as if she were skimming across space rather than walking. She sucked the lemon drop. Swallowed. Repeating the actions until her vision began to clear.

"Here, Vonnie. Drink it." Monique pulled Vonnie upright and held the orange juice to her mouth.

Vonnie took a large gulp of the juice, waited a few seconds, then took another sip. The world began to return to normal. She checked the lunchroom door and it looked as it always had looked, wide and open. Setting the juice cup aside, she rested her head on the table. A narrow escape. "Thanks, Monique. Thanks."

"Are you going to be okay? Shall I get help?"

"I'm fine. Just need to rest."

By now a crowd of curious students had begun to gather, and Vonnie heard Monique take charge.

"Stand back, everyone. Give her air. She's just stressed out and she needs space. Stand back." Then she turned to Vonnie again. "Can you stand up?"

"I think so." Vonnie raised her head and took a firm grip on the edge of the table as she tried to pull herself to her feet.

Monique cupped a hand under Vonnie's elbow, giving her support. "Let's head for the nurse's station. There's a cot there." Hurriedly she jammed Vonnie's scattered possessions back into her purse, then picked up the orange juice and carried it along.

The gaping crowd parted to let them through, and Vonnie leaned heavily on Monique's arm as they walked the short distance to the nurse's office.

"Nurse! Nurse!" Monique called, but nobody replied.

"Orange juice," Vonnie said. "More juice, please."

Monique gave her the cup, and she finished drinking the juice before she stretched out on the narrow cot beside the wall. Monique covered her with a blanket.

"I'll find the nurse," Monique said.

Vonnie could only nod. The softness of the cot, the warmth of the blanket were like luxuries. As soon as Monique left the room, Vonnie closed her eyes and felt herself drifting toward sleep. But almost immediately Monique returned.

"Vonnie, I can't find the nurse. I've looked everywhere. Tish saw her and Mr. Buckner taking some kid away in the school van. There must have been another emergency."

Vonnie sat up slowly. "I feel a lot better, Monique." She eased the blanket aside and swung her feet to the floor.

"You can't go back to class," Monique said. "What if you have another..."

"I'll call Mom." Vonnie looked at the telephone, but she didn't try to stand.

Monique poised her finger over the telephone on the nurse's desk. "What's your number? I'll dial for you."

Monique held the receiver toward Vonnie so she could hear the phone ringing, but nobody answered.

"She's probably out painting," Vonnie said.

"I'll drive you home." Monique pulled her car keys from her purse. "Let's split. Come on. My car's close to the door. Can you make it to the parking lot?"

"Of course," Vonnie said. "I'm feeling much better now. But whenever this happens, I'm supposed to rest for a while."

No teacher accosted them as they walked to the parking lot, got into Monique's car and headed toward Piney Glen. Vonnie's mother was still out, and Vonnie settled down on the living-room couch.

"Monique, thanks for helping. I could have been in serious trouble." Vonnie hesitated. "And I was scared. I've had these spells lots of times before, but they're always scary. That part of it never seems to change."

"You frightened me, too." Monique took a chair near the couch as if she had no intention of leaving Vonnie alone, and when she spoke, her voice was very low. "I'm sorry I accused you of faking it Friday night, Vonnie. Really sorry."

Vonnie drew a deep breath. "A couple of times when I felt boxed in, I did fake illness." She smiled sheepishly. "Friday was one of those times. So now you know. I'm really embarrassed about it." Vonnie closed her eyes, wishing Monique would go on home. She was grateful for her help, but she wasn't up to talking with her any longer.

"Right now, knowing that you've faked some attacks doesn't matter to me as much as it once did," Monique said. "In fact, it hardly matters at all. Had I been in your place, it's something I might have done, too."

When Vonnie didn't reply, Monique spoke again. "What's with us, anyway, Vonnie? I mean, we like each other. I know we do. Yet at the same time we dislike each other. Maybe we're getting flaky."

"I don't think so." Vonnie opened her eyes. "We're opposites in many ways. Sometimes I feel uncomfortable and bummed out when I'm around you, yet I admire your... your looks, your life-style, your neat French clothes." She hesitated, wondering if she would regret this openness later. Rather lamely she added, "And maybe there are a few things about me that you admire, too."

Why had she said that! That was really asking for it. So Monique had helped her out of a jam. That certainly didn't mean that Monique had changed her opinion of her or that she admired her. She closed her eyes again, wishing Monique would go away.

For a few moments Monique remained silent, then she nodded and sighed. "You're right. You bug me, but down deep I admire your leadership abilities, your good grades, your family."

"Family?" Vonnie's eyes popped open again.

"Your family that really cares about you."

Vonnie saw a sudden proud lift of Monique's chin that told her the admiration society had ended. "We'll probably never be soul mates or even best friends, Monique. We're too different for that. But I think we're beginning to understand each other. For the first time I sense a lot of empathy between us."

"Agreed. I'm beginning to know where you're coming from." Monique stood. "Can I bring you anything before I go?"

"No, I'm fine."

"Maybe I should stay with you until your mother gets here."

"No need. I'll nap for a few minutes, then I'll be back to normal. No big deal."

Monique let herself out the front door as Vonnie again closed her eyes.

On Tuesday all plans for the club meeting were go. The house was ready. Lora and Cass were bringing the refreshments, and Monique had the writing samples organized and ready for examination and discussion. Vonnie had been almost too busy to think about the lingering rift between her and Bob, but she had to face it head-on when both boys showed up after school to walk home with her.

Chet carried her books and walked on her right. Bob strolled along with them on Vonnie's left, stepping aside or dropping behind them when other people approached.

"You're both attending the meeting tonight, aren't you?" Vonnie asked, trying to keep the conversation on neutral ground. "If the discussion lags, I'm depending on you two to speak up."

"I'll make sure I'm in a talk mode," Bob said.

"What are Lora and Cass bringing to eat, Bob? Have they given you a peek?"

"They won't tell me," Bob said. "Top secret."

"Big deal," Chet said. "Why don't we just hang out at a burger joint afterward? Everyone could order what he wants."

"Lora and Cass volunteered," Vonnie said. "You can go out after you eat their refreshments, if you want to."

"Is it a date?"

Vonnie felt Chet looking directly at her, putting her on the spot.

"Afraid I can't make it, Chet. It'll be fairly late before the meeting ends, and I promised Mom I'd clean up any mess we might make."

Would they never reach her house! Fleetingly Vonnie envied Monique. Monique would enjoy the rapt attention of two boys.

When they reached her front door, Vonnie smiled and faced them with the doorknob pressing into her back. "See you two tonight. Remember, seven o'clock."

"Right," Chet said. "See you."

"Yeah," Bob said. "Seven."

She took her books from Chet, went inside and closed the door. And she didn't even peek out to see if the boys walked away together or if they went in different directions. After she ate her afternoon snack, she began setting up card tables.

Tonight they wouldn't need room for individual writing as they had last time. They would just be looking at the samples Monique was bringing. They might need to huddle together in order to see. Some could sit on the floor. The telephone interrupted her plans.

"Bob here, Vonnie. And I'm logging in in an apologetic mode. Will you read my file?"

"You've nothing to apologize for, Bob."

"Consider last Friday night. I'm sorry I accused you of being jealous of Monique. I'm sorry I let you get home on your own. My screen flashed me an error message almost immediately."

"Chet didn't mind driving me home."

"I know. All too well. I behaved like a real wimp, and I hope you'll forgive me and hit the delete command where Chet's concerned."

Vonnie smiled at Bob's attempt to cover the seriousness of his request with computer terms. "We're friends, Bob. Nothing's going to change that, but thanks for calling. I appreciate it."

"See you tonight, Vonnie."

"Right. I'm looking forward to it."

The club members began gathering a little before seven. All the original group arrived, along with ten new members. The living room and dining area were full, but there was no need for the patio.

"Dick!" Rod shouted. "You've grown hair. How'd you do it?"

All eyes turned to Dick's full head of hair.

"I used magic," Dick said, basking in their attention. "I bought this bottle of sparkling potion, rubbed it on my head and—presto, chango. Hair."

"You're kidding," Bob said. "It's a trick."

"Right," Dick agreed. "It is." Gleefully he reached up and pulled off a very natural-looking wig.

"Put it back on," Bob said. "Try to look normal."

Vonnie passed out slips of paper, waiting for everyone to quiet down. "Let's vote on a club name first. Write one choice on your slip and I'll collect them when you're finished."

She waited until everyone had stopped writing, then Bob helped her collect the slips. "Monique, you and Chet be tellers, please."

"Hurry up," Cass said. "Let's get on to the good stuff."

After the ballots had been counted, Monique faced the group. "The club name will be The Write Gang, Lora's original choice last week."

Everyone cheered, and when they stopped, Vonnie said, "A good name for a good club. Now we're going to get down to the business of looking at some writing samples and seeing what hidden messages we can read in them. Monique, show us the first sample, please."

"Here it is, gang." Monique stood before the group. "This writing came from one of our esteemed faculty members. I've made copies for everyone."

"Thanks, Monique." Vonnie spoke above the rustle of the paper. Then, turning to the group, she continued, "You learned last time how to look for overall personality traits, optimism, pessimism, energy and so forth. Always notice those things first as you examine a person's writing. Tonight, after noting the overall view, I want you to study the letter *t*."

"What if we missed the last meeting?" a boy called out.

"You can review my textbook during refreshment time," Vonnie said. "Or you can get the old members to help you."

"What shall we look for in the letter *t*?" Cass asked.

"Size first," Vonnie said. "That's usually a good starting point when you're studying any letter. Size. If it's a small simple letter, it indicates a balanced person of average intelligence."

"Forget that," Dick said. "None of our faculty is either of those things."

"Be serious, Dick," Cass said. "Hush up and listen."

"If the *t* stem is looped, it could mean the writer is oversensitive. If it's pointed, that could show bluntness. Someone tell me what you see so far. Rod?"

"The *t*'s vary in size, but most of them are small. None of them are looped. Many of them are pointed."

"Good. Keep those things in mind. Balance. Intelligence. Bluntness. Now look at the cross bars. A high cross means strong will. A low cross shows someone who usually submits to others."

"What about a cross halfway up?" Lora asked.

"That could show a calm and thoughtful person," Vonnie said. "If the cross is above the letter, it may mean the person is dominating and demanding. If the cross is to the left of the letter, it could indicate hesitation, but a cross to the right of the letter usually shows initiative."

"You're going too fast," Dick said.

"Hush and listen," Cass hissed.

"What do you see in this sample, Randy?"

"I see several things. Many high crosses. Many crosses to the right of the letter."

"So we have a strong-willed person and a person with initiative," Vonnie said, refreshing their minds. "Ready to take any guesses on who did the writing? We have *t*'s that show balance, intelligence, bluntness, a strong will, some initiative. Who does it remind you of?"

"Coach Henry," Tish said.

"No way," Randy said. "He doesn't have a well-balanced personality. He's too gung ho to win the games."

"It's got to be Mr. Buckner," Cass said. "Supposedly he's balanced and intelligent, and for sure he's blunt."

"Right," Bob agreed. "And he's certainly strong willed. Have any of you ever talked him out of anything?"

"He shows lots of initiative, too," Monique said. "He's designed punishments you'd never believe."

"So is the writing Buckner's?" Chet asked.

"It belongs to Mr. Adams, the music director," Vonnie said.

When everyone groaned, she smiled. "Don't give up. There are lots of letters to examine yet."

The group examined four more samples, guessing two of them correctly and two incorrectly.

"Now for the secret friend samples," Vonnie said. "I've chosen one to look at first.

"And I've made lots of copies." Monique passed out samples.

"Look at the basic characteristics of the writing first," Vonnie said. "Then review the *t*'s, trying to remember our discussion of that letter. Once you've done those things, we're going to study the letter *i*."

"I can't remember all this stuff," Dick said. "It goes in one head and out the other."

"That figures," Bob said.

"Just do your best to draw on what you already know as you learn more," Vonnie said.

"Circle dots indicate immaturity," Cass said "Right?"

"They merely indicate a young person," Monique said, flinging her hair over her shoulder. "Isn't that right, Vonnie? Isn't that what you told me once before?"

"That's a point where you'll sometimes have to use your own judgment whether a person is young or immature," Vonnie said. "Now hear this. A dot to the left of the letter *i* shows a slow thinker, while a dot to the right of the letter shows a quick mind. If the dot is shaped like a comma, that also indicates mental ability."

"What about no dot at all?" Bob asked.

"Indicates negligence. A light dot shows a person who may be easily influenced, and a dot shaped like an upside down *v* indicates eagerness. Anyone ready to describe the writer?"

Cass raised her hand. "I am."

"Go for it," Bob said, grinning. "Let's hear it."

"One question first," Cass said. "What does it indicate when the writing lines are almost level, but with just a few ups and downs within the line?"

Vonnie flipped through some pages in the textbook, then held it up. "If it looks like this, if the wanderings are minor, then it could show a genius at work."

"Genius! Wow!" Cass exclaimed.

"Or at least it could show a person who has many talents in many different directions."

"Okay." Cass wound a strand of red hair around her forefinger as she continued speaking. "I see all of that, and I also see *t* crosses that indicate initiative and some that indicate bluntness. I see some *i* dots that show a quick mind and eagerness."

"Good work," Vonnie said.

"I'm going to tell you who the writer is," Cass said.

"No fair," Randy called out. "This is supposed to be a secret friend. Secret!"

"But the sample is one I brought," Cass said. "And I want you to know who the writer is. He's agreed to go public."

"Who? Who?" The chorus came from everyone.

"Okay," Cass said. "Are you ready for this? The writer is Dick Randall."

"You're kidding," Bob said.

"The writing is Dick's," Cass said.

"And here I was beginning to believe this graphology stuff," Bob groaned.

"You've got a big mouth," Dick said. "Your trouble is you don't recognize genius when you see it."

"If you're a genius, you're right," Bob said. "I don't recognize it. I think your file has been misprogrammed."

"We all have individual personality and character traits," Vonnie said. "It's what we do with them that counts."

"What's that supposed to mean?" Dick pulled his wig over his left ear, basking in the laughter that followed.

"Well, for instance, a person may be clever, but it's up to him as to how he'll use all that cleverness."

"He could program it to rob banks," Bob said.

"Or he could use it to help solve community problems," Rod said.

"They mean you could use all that genius to irritate people," Cass said, looking at Dick. "Or you could use it in some better way."

"Big deal," Dick said. "Big, big deal."

"Let's go on to the next writing." Monique began passing out a second sheet of paper.

The evening passed smoothly and quickly. At nine o'clock everyone was ready to lay aside all writing samples and enjoy the sandwiches and punch Lora and Cass had prepared. The group spread out to the patio, but Vonnie and Bob sat in the kitchen.

"Good meeting, Vonnie," Bob said. "It almost went off the screen when Cass revealed Dick's identity, but it came back clear."

"Cass thinks Dick needs to know that he has a lot of potential. Somewhere along the way he's overlooked that fact."

"It's easy to overlook, I'd say."

"You're prejudiced." Vonnie laughed.

As soon as they finished eating, the group began to leave. Monique and Randy left first and Vonnie knew they were probably going with Chet and Tish to a burger joint. Dick and Cass were two of the last to leave.

"Had a neat time, Vonnie," Dick said.

"Thanks for your cooperation tonight, Dick. You made it a more interesting evening."

"Excuse me a minute, Vonnie." Dick disappeared into the bathroom and when he returned he was wearing his wig neatly in place. "Think I just might wear this hairpiece until my own hair grows out. It won't take long. I mean, a genius shouldn't be running around in a Mohawk, should he?"

"I wouldn't think so, Dick," Vonnie said, keeping her tone serious and respectful.

"Come on, Dick," Cass said. "It's been a big evening."

Vonnie watched them leave, knowing that Dick might or might not change his hairstyle, but also knowing that this graphology session had made him do some thinking. It had made her do some careful thinking, too. She and Monique had spent a whole evening together without insulting each other, without any ripples of conflict spilling out to spoil the meeting. She wondered if Monique had noticed that, too.

Eleven

After most of the kids had left the meeting, Vonnie and Lora straightened up the house, picking up papers, folding the card tables, cleaning the kitchen. A soft breeze blowing through the open patio door cooled them as they worked.

"It was a good meeting, Vonnie," Lora said. "Everyone had fun, and I think the new members were really impressed as well as entertained."

"I hope you're right. Three of the girls have ordered their own graphology texts. That shows more than a casual interest."

Vonnie snapped off the kitchen lights and walked to the living-room door with Lora.

"When your next article appears in the school paper, even more kids will want to join us. Are we going to set a limit?"

"Don't see why we should. The more kids, the more fun. Want me to drive you home?" Vonnie asked.

"No thanks. It's such a quiet night. I'll enjoy a few minutes of silence. See you tomorrow."

Vonnie left the porch light on and watched until Lora was in the next block where her own porch light was burning. Some evening. She felt pleased. No, she felt more than pleased. She felt elated, and she was far too excited to go to sleep.

Once in her room, she began making notes for her next graphology article while she was still filled with enthusiasm. Cass's idea wasn't too bad. She tried basing a short article on each letter of the alphabet, but before long that approach grew tedious and she searched for a new slant.

She was still thinking about the article, or a series of articles, when she reached homeroom the next morning.

"Great meeting last night," Randy said as he passed in front of her to reach his chair. "Graphology is the big topic this morning. Everyone's trying to get writing samples from their friends."

"I'm communicating on computer only," Bob said. "Don't want everyone analyzing me."

"You guys could use some tips on how to write like a genius," Dick said. "I'm selling samples of my writing. Any takers?"

Vonnie smiled at Dick, noticing that he was still wearing his wig and that it looked natural. She wondered how long it would take his hair to grow out.

As Monique entered the room, Mr. Buckner's voice blared over the intercom.

"Will Vonnie Morrison please report to the school office? Vonnie Morrison to the office, please."

"Uh-oh," Cass said. "What did you do?"

"Nothing that I know of," Vonnie said.

"Well, don't just sit there," Cass said. "Go and find out."

"Want a genius to escort you?" Dick asked.

Vonnie picked up her books and headed out the door, hurrying down the hallway to the principal's office. Maybe someone had complained about the club meeting. She was still mulling over possibilities as she entered the main office, stepping around three boys waiting for tardy slips and a girl who had forgotten the combination to her lock. Standing in the doorway of his private office, Mr. Buckner motioned her inside.

"Vonnie," Mr. Buckner said, adjusting his tie, which didn't need adjusting, "I want you to meet Hank Durell from *The Houston Post*. He's asked to talk with you about a business matter."

"Hank, this is Vonnie Morrison. Please feel free to use my office for your discussion."

"Thanks Mr. Buckner," Hank said.

Hank Durell. The name sounded slightly familiar to Vonnie, but she couldn't quite place it. She guessed Hank to be in his late twenties and she liked his looks. Slim. Rangy. His brown cord slacks and his tweed jacket with the leather elbow patches went well with his red hair and freckles and his friendly blue eyes.

"Vonnie," Hank said, "I've read the graphology article you wrote for your school paper and I liked it very much."

"Thank you." What did this man want? It must be something important or Mr. Buckner wouldn't let him use his office and take school time to talk with her.

"Are you taking journalism this semester?"

"No, sir. I'm in a college prep program that only includes journalism if I choose it as an elective."

"And you haven't done that?"

"No. At least not this semester."

"What else have you written?"

"Nothing. I mean, of course I write my school lessons. English themes. History papers. That sort of thing."

"But you haven't done other writing for publication?"

"No, I really haven't."

"That's quite unusual. Your article shows writing ability. It shows a natural feel for words and their usage."

"Thank you." What was he getting at? She wished she could sit down, but no one had mentioned that. Knowing she would feel uneasy sitting as long as he was standing, she shifted her weight from one foot to the other, her books from one arm to the other.

"Would you let us reprint your graphology article in *The Post*, Vonnie? I always keep an eye out for new writers, and school papers are one of the places where I sometimes find new talent. Your article grabbed me right away."

Talent. She could bliss out on the word. Talent.

"We would pay you a small fee for reprint rights," Hank Durell said. "Not much, mind you. But some. And you'd have your own byline, of course."

Pay. Byline. Talent. The ideas overwhelmed her.

"Of course, if you're not interested . . ."

Vonnie found her voice. "Oh, I'm interested. I'm just so surprised I don't know what to say."

"Try saying yes and see how it sounds to you," he suggested.

"Yes. Yes, I'd really be pleased to have you reprint my article. When? When will it be in the paper?"

"Perhaps tomorrow, if I can arrange it. If not, then the next day."

"That's exciting," Vonnie said. "I had no idea anyone would be interested in my writing. Anyone besides Miss Hunt and the kids here at school, I mean."

"I've talked to Miss Hunt," Hank said. "Talked with her on the telephone before I came to see Mr. Buckner. She tells me you may do a series of articles. Is that right?"

"I'm considering it," Vonnie said.

"I'd be interested in seeing anything else you write, especially if it's on the subject of graphology."

"I'll be glad to show you my articles," Vonnie said, deciding then and there to do the series.

"Now, I'm not saying we'll buy all of them," Hank said, "but there's a good chance we'll be interested in some of them if they're as well written as your first one. We'll be in touch."

"Thank you," Vonnie said. "Thank you."

"You'll receive a check in the mail shortly after publication of your article. It's been fun talking with you Vonnie. We journalists have a lot in common."

Opening the door, Hank Durell let Vonnie leave first, and she watched him as he walked down the hall and headed toward the exit. She stood in the corridor for a few moments after he left, still surprised at his request. Hank Durell thought she had talent. She had been published in her school paper and now she was to be published in the city paper. Great! She liked the idea very much. Maybe this was the goal she had been seeking. Perhaps writing was the thing she could throw her energies into in a way that could lead to an important career. Writing. Why hadn't she thought of it sooner?

When Vonnie returned to homeroom, her friends looked at her questioningly, but she avoided their eyes, keeping her attention on announcements that were being made and then on her assignments. Later, when she stepped into the hall, Lora was at her side in a minute.

"What did Buckner want? Give. What's up?"

"He just wanted to talk to me some more about the graphology article."

"Oh." Lora sounded disappointed. "He liked it okay, didn't he? No problems?"

"No problems. He was just . . . interested." Why was she holding back? She hated keeping secrets from Lora, but she wasn't ready to tell her news to anyone just yet. She wanted more time to think about it herself, to dream about it, to wonder about it. Sharing the news could come later.

By lunchtime everyone seemed to have forgotten that she had been called to the office, and Vonnie said nothing to remind them. Dick talked about his wig.

"It itches so I took it off," he said. "Can't stand it."

"Try," Cass said. "It'll be worth a little itch to look normal again."

"Normal. Normal. Who's to say what's normal? Kids don't wear wigs. Anyway, it doesn't go with my new car."

"What new car?" Cass asked. "I didn't know anything about a new car."

"I haven't put any money on it yet, but it's down at Ace's Used Car Emporium. It's painted a neat shade of orange. Mag wheels. Oversize rears. It'll go from zero to sixty in ten seconds."

"Wonderful," Cass said. "Sounds like a perfect match for your Mohawk!" Then she sighed. "Dick, how can you?"

"It's easy. You'll see. Just as soon as I raise the seven thou."

"Seven thousand!" Cass said. "You've flipped. But how about promising me one thing?"

"What?"

"Promise that wig or no wig you'll let your hair grow until you raise the seven thou."

Vonnie ignored the dispute between Cass and Dick. Dick would probably use the wig as an attention getter, but maybe he would let his hair grow. It was a possibility.

It pleased Vonnie that Bob had claimed a place beside her at the table again. Chet was sitting beside Tish and a new girl Tish had introduced him to. Vonnie wondered what the new girl's handwriting looked like.

After school, Bob stood waiting at Vonnie's locker. "You going straight home?" he asked.

"Yes. Got lots of studying to do tonight. Math test. English paper. History assignment."

"Yeah, they really laid it on us today." They strolled on without talking for a while, then Bob began walking more slowly. "I've been wanting to ask you something, Vonnie."

"What?" Vonnie asked, preparing to explain about the call to the office.

"We've never talked about going steady, but we have been going steadily. Right?"

"Right. We have."

"It really bothered me last Friday to see you leave Tut's Tomb with Chet. And it bothered me even more to see you sit with him in the lunchroom on Monday."

"I've never been really pleased to see you with Tish, either," Vonnie admitted.

"So how about going steady?" Bob asked. "What do you think?"

Vonnie was thinking so many things that she didn't know what to say first, but she knew she must consider carefully before she spoke. Why hadn't she told Bob about Hank Durell and his offer concerning her article? Surely a girl should want her nearly steady boyfriend to know about the good things that happened in her life. But for some reason she wasn't ready to tell Bob just yet.

"Are you still angry because I said you were jealous of Monique?" Bob asked.

"No. You were right, you know. I do get a little green eyed when I'm around her."

"And I think she's envious of you, too," Bob said. "You usually handle your feelings better than she does." Bob hesitated, then he spoke again. "You really don't want to go steady with me, do you?"

"It's not that I don't want to go steady with you, Bob. It's just that I'm really not ready to go steady with anyone right now."

"You've got a boyfriend somewhere else?"

"I've lived in lots of towns and cities, Bob. And yes, I know nice guys in most of them."

"Did you go steady with them?"

"No." Vonnie laughed. "I never lived in one spot long enough to go steady. After a few months Dad would be transferred. Or sometimes the guy I was dating would move."

"You still write to those guys?"

"Yes. And I still write to girls I knew in those towns, too. Sometimes I miss old friends a great deal. If we left Houston, I'd miss the friends I've made here, too."

"Okay, Vonnie. So you don't want to go steady. But you will keep on going out with me, won't you?"

"Of course. I'll look forward to it. But we both need to meet others, to get to know a variety of people."

When they reached Vonnie's house, Vonnie invited Bob in, but he headed on home and she felt relieved. She wanted to be alone. Just for a while she needed time to think and to sort out her thoughts.

She felt as if she had the most interesting secret in the whole world. Vonnie Morrison, professional writer. She could make it real. At least she could give it her best shot and see what happened. Two people thought she had talent. Miss Hunt. Mr. Durell. And of course her parents thought so, but they were prejudiced in her favor.

Closing her eyes, she pictured her byline in the school paper. And she pictured it again in the city paper. Would anyone notice it? Many times she read articles without ever noticing who wrote them. From now on she would pay more attention to bylines.

Why hadn't she told Bob about the offer from Hank Durell? Or Lora? She didn't even feel in the mood to write the good news to Pete or Hannah or Chuck.

As dusk began to fall, she knew who she must share her secret with first. Monique. Strange that it should be Monique who certainly wasn't her very best friend. Monique might even laugh at her. But she remembered the time when Monique first realized she wanted to be an actress and had shared her dreams with her. She hadn't laughed at Monique. Now it was time for Monique to return the favor. But would she?

She looked up Wagar in the telephone directory, dialed Monique's number and waited.

"Wagar residence." Glady's voice came over the wire.

Wrong number. Carefully Vonnie hung up. She didn't want Glady to call Monique to the telephone. She looked in the directory again, searching until she found Monique's private teen telephone number. She dialed again.

"Hello," Monique said.

Vonnie gulped, swallowed, then almost hung up a second time.

"Hello?" Monique said. "Who is it?"

"It's Vonnie, Monique. I've got something to tell you."

"I'm listening. All signals are go."

"It's about my graphology article. I haven't told anyone else because I wanted you to be the first to know."

"I'm still listening."

"A man from *The Post* came to talk to me today. Hank Durell. That's why Mr. Buckner called me to the office this morning. Monique, he's going to reprint my article in the city paper."

"My handwriting's going to be in *The Post*?" Monique asked. "Really, Vonnie? My writing?"

"Your handwriting and *my article*," Vonnie said. "Monique, I'm thinking about being a writer. I'm considering it as a career."

She waited. If Monique laughed, if she said one more word about her own handwriting, she would hang up.

"Vonnie, that's terrific. You'll make a great writer. Maybe you can write my reviews when I'm a famous actress."

"Could be."

"Let's talk about it, huh?" Monique said. "Could you come over tonight? Sleep over, I mean, so we can really talk in private. We've got plans to make."

"I've got studying to do tonight," Vonnie said.

"Yeah, well." Monique hesitated. "If you come over we could . . . study together."

"You mean it?"

"Of course I mean it. An actress needs some smarts. Maybe it's time I started trying to live up to all that potential you're always seeing in my writing. We'll study together then we'll talk about our careers."

"Okay, Monique."

"Oh, Vonnie, I'm so glad you told me the big news first. I'm really flattered. You're the W-R-I-T-E kind of girl, Von."

After they finished talking, Vonnie replaced the receiver and started packing her overnight case. How had this happened? She knew she and Monique would never be best friends. They were too different for that. Maybe they were riding for another fall. And maybe not. They had learned a lot about each other in the few short weeks they had been acquainted. There was a degree of understanding between them. And Vonnie sensed a mutual admiration. Tonight, at least, they were just two friends who were going to talk about their careers. Monique might not be the nicest person she had ever met, but for sure she was one of the most interesting. Who could ask for more than that? Maybe the best was yet to come.

Was Vonnie right?
Look for *Vonnie and Monique*
by Dorothy Francis
Now partners and friends,
the two girls
take on life and love
with some surprising results.
A Keepsake, of course.

GUYS, DATING AND OTHER DISASTERS
by
Arlene Erlbach

My mom died when I was seven. Last year my dad met Joy Kellison, my future stepmother, at a University of Chicago alumni party. They're getting married in a few weeks, and I'm going to be the maid of honor.

Ricky Fingerbaum is my first boyfriend. We haven't exactly experienced 303 blissfully romantic days. He has never whispered sweet anythings in my ear or even sent me a valentine.

As soon as I wake up, I hear the phone ring. "Henny!" my father calls. "This one is a real looney tune! He wants to talk to his *beautiful wife*. Can't you find a normal boy to date at that high school?"

All excerpts from GUYS, DATING
AND OTHER DISASTERS.

GUYS-1-BPA

ATTRACTIVE, SPACE SAVING BOOK RACK

Display your most prized novels on this handsome and sturdy book rack. The hand-rubbed walnut finish will blend into your library decor with quiet elegance, providing a practical organizer for your favorite hard-or soft-covered books.

Only $9.95

Approximately 16" x 8" when assembled

Assembles in seconds!

To order, rush your name, address and zip code, along with a check or money order for $10.70* ($9.95 plus 75¢ postage and handling) payable to *Crosswinds*.

Crosswinds
Book Rack Offer
901 Fuhrmann Blvd.
P.O. Box 1396
Buffalo, NY 14269-1396

Offer not available in Canada.

*New York residents add appropriate sales tax.

BKR-3